Weekly Reader Children's Book Club Presents

Puppy Lost in Lapland

Puppy Lost
in Lapland

by PETER HALLARD

ILLUSTRATED BY
Wallace Tripp

Franklin Watts, Inc.
845 Third Avenue
New York, N.Y. 10022

Contents

Puppy Lost in Lapland

"*Lame pups are no use!*"

An older dog would have been far too wise to charge straight at a reindeer stag; but Veddge was only a six-month-old puppy. All morning he had been chasing around excitedly, helping to keep the big herd under control. Now, when it seemed as though this big stag were going to break free, he rushed at it.

Instead of turning away, the stag reared, then struck at the puppy with his big cloven hoofs. He brought them down with terrific force, and though Veddge tried to check his rush-in, the top layer of snow was half melted, and his paws skidded, causing him to slither helplessly forward.

Thump! The reindeer stag's forehoofs smashed deep into the snow, bringing a yelp of agony from the puppy. The hoofs had missed Veddge's head, but one had struck his foreleg a glancing blow. The stag did not know he had struck the puppy; but for Veddge the pain was like the thrust of a red-hot knife.

For the moment Veddge was unable to move, and the stag reared again to deliver a blow that would finish off the puppy. Just then an older dog charged in. Too wise to risk a frontal attack, the dog aimed at the shoulders. His weight threw the stag off balance, saving Veddge's life, for the cloven hoofs came down only on melting snow.

Seconds later the stag was being driven back into the herd while Veddge lay whimpering, holding his injured paw out of the snow. Anxiously he watched the movements of any reindeer that came near, afraid of being stepped on. Does, stags, and year-old calves were milling around. Since dawn it had taken a continuous effort by herdsmen and dogs to keep the reindeer from breaking out of the valley and heading north, for spring was in the air.

The long darkness of winter was past, and each day the sun rose earlier. There was growing warmth in it too. Water dripped off the frozen branches of the birch trees, the surface of the snow was softening, and there was even a narrow black lane down the center of the stream which had been frozen solid all winter.

Daily the reindeer grew more restless, and this morning old Johan, who owned the herd, decided they would leave for the northwest. When they reached the northern coast of Norway, he would swim his reindeer over to one of the offshore islands. There they could enjoy peace and quiet for two or three months.

It was the roundup of the herd that had made Veddge so excited, for he sensed it meant they would be on the move. Now he lay helpless in the wet snow while the herd was moved nearer the campsite. He whined and tried to stand, but his right foreleg was so painful he could not move in the slushy snow. He could hear his fourteen-year-old master, Aslak, shouting now and then, but the boy never came close enough to hear Veddge's anxious barking.

The puppy had been given the unusual Lapp name of Veddge (Fetch) because almost from the day he could tumble about, he would rush to the tent door when Aslak's mother, Susannan, shouted *veddge chadzi* (fetch water), or *veddge morre* (fetch wood). It seemed as if the word *veddge* always brought the puppy to his feet, ready and anxious to dash after Aslak.

They even teased him when he was dozing by whispering the word *veddge*. Then his ears would prick, and a second later he would be on his feet. Finally, Aslak's mother suggested that Veddge might be a good name for him since he seemed to understand it so well.

It was Aslak who found Veddge almost an hour after the accident. Realizing the puppy was missing, he went searching, skiing up the valley until he saw the little dark bundle of wet fur half hidden in the snow. Anxiously he called: "Now, what's the matter with you? Up, Veddge, up!"

Veddge got shakily to his feet, his right paw held out. Aslak's eyes narrowed as he realized that something serious had happened. Slipping his reindeer-skin shoes out of his ski loops, he knelt and took the injured paw in his hands. Feeling the puppy cringe, he let the paw rest on one gloved hand while he took a closer look.

"Don't say it's broken," he muttered. "If it is, that'll be the end of you." Scooping up a handful of snow, he pressed it gently on the swollen foreleg, and as Veddge

§ 13

whimpered, he murmured: "All right, I'm trying to help. I don't want to hurt you. Keep still."

Aslak spread the wet snow gently along the leg, at the same time trying to feel if there was a broken bone. When he finally released the paw, there was sorrow in his voice as he murmured: "And I was hoping you would grow up into the best reindeer dog we'd ever had. Now . . . ." and he shook his head. In the wilderness of Lapland, dogs were not kept as pets. They were work dogs, kept to herd the reindeer and guard them against attack by wolves or the occasional wolverine.

Gently lifting Veddge out of the snow, he carried him down the valley and through the milling herd of reindeer to their encampment. It was a hut with tiny windows and a stone chimney. Near the door were the *pulkkas* (small boat-shaped sledges). Aslak's mother, Susannan, was busy packing her household things in the *pulkkas*. They had to be ready at sunset, for then the frost would have returned and the wet snow would have frozen again. A firm surface on the snow was essential if reindeer were to draw the laden *pulkkas* any distance.

"What's the matter with him?" Susannan asked, pausing for a moment.

"Feel his leg," Aslak suggested. "I think he must have been trodden on. It's very swollen. Do you think it is broken?"

Susannan was just going to feel the swollen foreleg when her father, Aslak's grandfather, swung round the side of the hut on his skis. Aslak's father was dead, so old

Johan was always a busy man. His eyes missed nothing, and without a word he came over, felt Veddge's leg for a moment, and then grunted: "I always said that puppy wouldn't live to grow up into a dog. Too crazy keen. It feels as if the bone is broken. Get rid of him, Aslak. Even if the bone sets, he won't be any good for herding. Lame pups are no use!" Turning away, he went into the hut.

Aslak opened his mouth to protest, but even his mother had turned away. There was so much to do before the sun set, and the dog was Aslak's worry. He looked at Veddge, and the puppy reached up and tried to lick his cheek. It brought a lump to Aslak's throat. "Get rid of him." That was what grandfather Johan had ordered. "Get rid of him!" That meant—*kill him!*

He heard his grandfather moving in the hut and hurried round the back. Old Johan was one of the best reindeer men in Lapland—everyone said that—and what he did not know about reindeer and reindeer dogs was hardly worth knowing.

Fondling the whimpering puppy until his grandfather had gone off again, Aslak then went to ask his mother's advice. She was packing the big wooden box which always went with them. It contained all her treasures—among them some real china crockery which Aslak's father had bought for her soon after they were married. There were her needles and thread, her coffee grinder, and a beautifully carved cheese mold she would use when the reindeer does were giving more milk than the calves needed.

"I know what you are going to say," Susannan said

when Aslak came up. "You have always thought too much of that pup. Anyway, your grandfather has told you what to do—go and do it. He won't let you keep a lame pup. When you've got rid of him, you can come and give me a hand with the packing. There are herdsmen to feed as well as you and your grandfather, and I have only one pair of hands."

Sadly Aslak carried the puppy round the back of the hut. He had to do something about Veddge at once. There *was* plenty of work to do, for the moment the surface of the snow had frozen hard enough, the hut door would be made fast and the herd would be allowed to start north. Once the trek began, there would be no time to think of injured puppies, for their way led across a high fell—the most dangerous part of the trip.

"But if there is no time to look *after* him," Aslak murmured, a sudden gleam of hope in his eyes, "there will be no time to look *for* him. If I could hide him in one of the *pulkkas*, his leg might have begun to heal before mother sees him again."

He looked round the end of the hut. Several reindeer were tethered close by. They had been trained to drag the laden *pulkkas*. Aslak's mother would ride in the first one; the reindeer drawing the second *pulkka* would be fastened by a fifteen-foot leather strap to the back of the first, so he could not stray. The second *pulkka* was already packed, piled high with the *peskes*, the warm reindeer-skin robes used only during the bitterest of wintry weather.

No one rode in the second *pulkka*. Cautiously lifting

the edge of one of the big reindeer robes, Aslak eased his puppy under it. He laid a warning finger on his lips. The puppy had already learned that this signal meant "silence." "You've got to keep quiet and still," Aslak warned. "If you are discovered, you could be dead by morning. Grandfather doesn't like useless dogs. Understand?"

Veddge merely looked at him; his injured leg was throbbing, but he made no sound as Aslak went into the hut. There he found a small roll of beautifully decorated braid. His mother had been busy making it throughout the winter, for the two-inch-wide braid was to decorate a new dress she was making. Aslak cut off two feet of the braid, then returned to where Veddge was lying under the edge of the reindeer-skin robe.

Scraping up some earth and snow, Aslak packed it against the pup's swollen leg, then bound it in place with the gaily decorated braid. "If mother sees this, Veddge," he whispered, "I'll be in trouble. So keep quiet, and keep out of sight. If your leg does get better, maybe she'll forgive my using the braid. So, if you want to help me, keep your leg still and give it a chance to heal." He patted the puppy gently, pulled the edge of the reindeer skin over Veddge's head, then moved away, whistling softly.

Aslak busied himself helping his mother pack. The moment they left this place, they would have no real roof over their heads at night. Whenever they halted, Aslak and his mother would erect their *kata* (tent), which was like a Red Indian tepee, and that would be their home until they returned next autumn to their winter hut.

From the moment Veddge was hidden until the sun set, Aslak was anxious. He knew that if either his mother or his grandfather discovered the injured puppy, they would not only be angry, but would insist on his getting rid of Veddge. A good dog was a treasure; but an untrained, injured puppy was useless.

As the sun sank to the horizon, Susannan called to Aslak, suggesting he go and see if his grandfather and the two herdsmen needed relief. Aslak shook his head, saying: "I think I'd better make sure we've packed everything. I have a feeling we shall have an early frost. If we do, grandfather may want to start before you are ready."

His mother laughed as she said: "You are very funny, Aslak. How do you think I managed while you were a baby? Then I had to do everything *and* keep an eye on you. As for our having an early frost—we might, but unless I am mistaken, we could have snow before morning. There's snow in the sky, snow and wind."

Aslak looked up and was worried. He was beginning to know something about clouds, and there *was* wind up there, if the clouds were telling the truth. He closed his eyes at the thought of what might happen if grandfather Johan decided there was a risk of a snowstorm and postponed the start of the trek. Veddge would be discovered, and that would be the end of him.

He looked anxiously northward to the high fell they must cross before they got to the coast. It looked gray in the fading light; gray and frightening. No one liked crossing that high ground, for storms could spring up very quickly, and once the reindeer started to cross, they had to keep going, for there was no shelter.

Turning, Aslak looked at the nearest stunted birches, and new hope came to him. The water which had been dripping from the twigs since soon after sunrise was now freezing; instead of dripping water there were icicles. He had been right. The temperature was dropping earlier than usual.

To his mother he said triumphantly: "You see, the frost is here already. I said it would be early. Now we can start. Grandfather should be here any minute."

"You seem very eager to be off," his mother said. "What's the matter with you? Have you done something you shouldn't have done?"

"You've been near enough to watch what I've been doing," Aslak said. "You should know if I've done something wrong."

His mother looked at him for a moment, but whatever she was going to say went unsaid, for just then one of the two herdsmen arrived. Slipping off his skis, he went into the hut for the food he knew would be waiting for him. As he pushed open the door, he said: "The master says we'll start as soon as possible. He'll be coming for coffee when I get back."

While his mother was pouring coffee for the herdsman, Aslak went out to the *pulkka* and tucked Veddge in after giving him a tidbit of meat he had smuggled out of the hut.

Not long afterward they were ready to move. Johan

and the second herdsman came along. They drank coffee and ate some reindeer meat. Then the big cooking pot was stowed on Susannan's *pulkka*. The fire was put out and they left the hut.

Darkness had fallen, and the stars were very bright, a sign of a hard frost. Aslak and his mother busied themselves harnessing the reindeer to the *pulkkas*. Johan, who because of his age also rode a *pulkka*, had already gone on. The dogs, who had been holding the herd in check, were called back. The two Lapp herdsmen made the night ring with their loud cries of *aw-awwww-aw-aw-aw!*

Somewhere up ahead the silence that followed was broken by the musical tonk-tonk of a bell slung around the neck of the largest of the stags. He was not only the largest, but also the wisest. He had made the journey over the fell seven times, and the rest of the reindeer were always willing to follow the sound of his bell.

Aslak checked the harness of the reindeer which would follow his mother's *pulkka*. Unlike the harness of a horse or a donkey, that of a reindeer is a single strap. This strap goes under the animal's chest, then between his front and back legs, and so to the attachment point on the *pulkka*. It is simple, but it works well with reindeer.

"Ready, Mother?" Aslak asked. When she said she was, Aslak drew away and slipped his curl-toed reindeer-skin shoes into the loops of his skis. His mother gave a twitch with the single rein, and the big reindeer made a leap forward. A moment later both *pulkkas* were being dragged at a gallop so wild that few people except a Lapp would have been able to retain their seat. A flock of snow sparrows, which had arrived from the south that morning and had perched side by side on the branches of a nearby birch tree, flew up in alarm at the commotion.

Aslak skied round their winter hut, making sure that nothing had been left behind. Though the sun had set over an hour ago, the stars were so bright that their reflected light on the snow made it quite easy to see anything. Satisfied that nothing had been left behind, Aslak began to ski after his mother.

In the first hour they covered seven miles, and then the initial enthusiasm of the herd petered out. They were beginning to climb the fell, and the speed dropped. In the next half hour a change came over the scene. It had been possible, because of the brilliance of the stars, to see things against the snow, and Aslak had had a view of the back of the second *pulkka* on which Veddge was lying.

But now clouds blew up from the west. Quickly they covered the sky, blotting out the stars and casting a deep blackness over everything. The pace of the reindeer slackened even more.

The herd had been spread out like a great arrowhead, with the tonk-tonk-tonk of the belled stag at the point of the arrow. Upon the thickening darkness, the reindeer drew closer together. Even the stags were nervous—and with good reason.

Three times during the past month wolves had attacked the herd. On the first two occasions they had killed a doe and a yearling calf. The third attack had been driven off, and a wolf had been killed. The end of the winter was the time to expect attacks, for there was little food, and starvation made the marauders doubly bold.

Herdsmen and dogs knew the danger too. The men skied round the herd, the dogs barking now and then to warn any nearby wolves that they could not hope to make a kill that night.

Slowly the herd climbed up to the top of the fell. There were no birch trees here, and very little of the snow had melted. Weeks would pass before the brown earth would begin to show. It was here that the last severe storm of the winter had suddenly blown up.

Screaming gusts of wind came out of the darkness, carrying fine snow which stung like leaden pellets. There was no shelter, and it would have been as dangerous to turn back as to go on. The herdsmen and the dogs kept the animals moving. With snow settling on their hides, even the darkest-colored reindeer were soon covered with white.

Young Veddge lay in the second *pulkka*, wrapped in the warmth of a reindeer robe. Occasionally he poked out his nose to sniff the bitterly cold air. The reindeer ahead were like ghosts, and the herdsmen, tough Lapps though they were, had to turn aside now and then to clear their eyes of snow.

No one could see clearly far ahead, and the reindeer kept as close to one another as possible. To stray now could mean death, for tracks were blotted out in seconds.

Aslak's mother could only sit hunched on her *pulkka* and trust to her reindeer to follow the herd. The leading reindeer stag, with the bell about its neck, was being urged along by one of the herdsmen. He had slipped a rope through the bell collar and was forcing the stag to move into the storm. The rest of the herd followed one another. Those who could hear the tonk-tonk-tonk of the bell kept as near to it as they could. Those behind were in an almost solid mass, bunched close so that they would not lose contact with the leader.

In that storm any man could be forgiven for getting off course, and the man leading the belled stag strayed too far to the north. He came dangerously close to a deep ravine, and it was more by luck than judgment that none of the herd slipped off the slope.

Susannan was so close to the ravine lip that the reindeer drawing the *pulkka* behind her actually put one hoof over the edge. For a second the *pulkka* also started to slide over the edge. With a startled bleat the reindeer gave a wild leap and jerked the *pulkka* to safety, and it was that sudden jerk that brought disaster to the unlucky puppy Veddge.

As he felt the *pulkka* beginning to slide sideways into the ravine, Veddge rose. He was balancing on his three strong legs, and when the *pulkka* was jerked back to safety, Veddge was unable to keep his balance and was tipped out. He gave a startled howl and a moment later was slithering helplessly down the slope. Susannan, who had never known that the injured puppy was in the second *pulkka*, gave a jerk with her single rein and guided her own reindeer more to the south, to firmer ground.

§ 24

Throughout the rest of that wild, snowy night, the herd struggled on. They reached the top of the fell, then started downward to the calmer regions of the valleys beyond. It was only when daylight came, about nine o'clock next morning, that Aslak went to the second *pulkka* to take some food to his puppy. Veddge was gone.

Sadly he turned to his mother, who was putting more meat into the pot over a fire she had just lit. He confessed what he had done. "I was sure the leg would mend," he insisted.

"They never mend," his mother said. "And with only three good legs, he will have died in that storm. Don't worry. There will be other puppies."

"But he was a good puppy," Aslak muttered.

"Forget him. He isn't worrying, Aslak," Susannan said gently. "By now he is dead."

"He might be following us—on three legs," Aslak said miserably. "He would try to follow us, I'm sure. He was that kind of a puppy. He never gave up."

His mother shook her head. "Not even a dog with four sound legs could follow us in that storm. And he's never been this way before, Aslak. It isn't any use worrying about him. Forget him. He's dead. I'm certain of that."

Susannan did not make many mistakes. But she was mistaken then, for the puppy was not dead—and, as Aslak said, *Veddge was not giving up.*

A lost puppy

Seconds after being tipped off the back of the *pulkka*, Veddge was almost swallowed up by the snow. He slid down the edge of the ravine and stopped only when the snow became too solid to allow him to slide farther. He barked and barked, trying to tell Aslak what had happened to him; but though the barking was like thunder in the puppy's ears, the snow smothered the sounds.

The storm raged on throughout the night, the wind howling and screaming as though it were a living thing. It seemed as if winter was using up the last of its strength to stop spring from coming.

If Veddge had been up there, he would have died, for with only three strong legs he could not have walked, and the cold would have frozen him to death. As it was, he lay under a blanket of snow and the wind did not get to him. The coolness of the snow on his injured foreleg was comforting. The bone was not broken, only cracked, and the chill took some of the fever out of the fracture.

A suggestion of light seeping through the snow persuaded the puppy to fight his way upward, and he found that morning had come. The storm clouds had gone, and a sun that looked like a lemon was shining from an almost clear sky.

Veddge howled in an effort to tell Aslak where he was. When no one came, he sniffed hopefully, but the snow had blotted out all the reindeer tracks, and there was not even the faintest scent to tell him which way they had gone. He was lost!

With no Aslak to give him orders, Veddge did not know what to do. Except when he was a very small puppy, and being fed by his mother, he had always been with Aslak. The Lapp boy had done everything: taught him what he had to do, fed him, patted him when he was good and punished him when he was disobedient.

Now there was no Aslak, no Lapp tent, no reindeer. Veddge was alone—lost on top of a great snow-covered fell. If he had turned northwest, he might have found Aslak before the day was over, for old Johan had decided to give the reindeer a day's rest after the struggle through the blizzard, and they were not so very far away. Unhappily for Veddge, he turned south.

Slowly he limped down the fell to the valley where they had been the previous day. The sun was once more melting the snow on the dwarf birch trees, and there was a black line down the center of the stream showing where the ice was melting. Veddge was hungry, but he dipped his muzzle into the icy water and drank.

He was starting to head downstream when he saw something moving about two hundred yards to the east.

§ 28

Thinking it must be one of the other herd dogs, he barked a greeting and started to limp forward, his eyes shining with hope.

Before he had gone a dozen yards, however, he stopped. There was something peculiar about this animal. It was shorter in the legs than any dog Veddge had seen. Nor was it a wolf. It was heavily built and approached with a peculiar waddling kind of gallop.

When the light breeze finally brought the stranger's scent to him, Veddge's eyes suddenly glowed bright green, and the thick ruff of hair on his neck and shoulders rose stiffly. The scent was one he had learned to hate and fear. The animal coming toward him was a wolverine.

One of the earliest lessons Veddge had learned was to hate wolverines even more than wolves or the occasional bear or lynx. The wolverine is a solitary hunter, a ferocious killer. What's more, it is absolutely fearless. If cornered by herd dogs, the wolverine will fight to the end and will certainly kill or maim several dogs before he is killed.

He is hated because of his cunning. When the snow is deep and the reindeer have dug lanes in the snow so that they can reach the hidden reindeer moss, the wolverine scurries along these lanes. He travels unseen by herdsmen or dogs, and before he is discovered, he may kill or maim several reindeer. His appetite is tremendous, and in some parts of the world he is known as the glutton. Now, this wolverine was coming toward Veddge; and after a long, hard winter, he was lean and very hungry.

When he realized Veddge was a dog, the wolverine

advanced more slowly. He was clever enough to know that where there was a dog there was usually a man, and he did not like man.

Circling the unhappy puppy, he sniffed the air, trying to get the scent of the men he hated; but there was no man scent in the cold, clean air. Finally, satisfied that this lean young puppy was really alone, he approached. His lips were drawn back in a soundless snarl, and he would have frightened a larger dog than Veddge.

Little shivers of fear ran through the lost puppy. Had he not been lame, he would have turned and run, though that would not have saved him. The wolverine is a tireless hunter, and Veddge would finally have been caught.

Knowing he could not run, Veddge began to back away, always facing his enemy. The wolverine was puzzled. He was not frightened, but he was wondering why this solitary puppy did not try to escape.

Slowly he began to walk toward Veddge, his heavy head only an inch or so from the snow. His powerful muscles were tightening for a spring. His mouth was slightly open, showing the wicked-looking teeth.

Veddge continued to limp backward until he could go no farther, for he was standing on ice. Behind him was the stream and the black lane where the ice had melted. He dared not turn to try to leap over the gap, for the wolverine was now only three yards away and gathering himself for a spring.

Growling deep in his throat and showing his teeth, Veddge tried to scare the wolverine away. It was a wasted

§ 30

effort. Suddenly, the squat figure rose from the snow in a tremendous leap, its eyes blazing, its stubby forepaws at full stretch.

Veddge showed his courage then, for he rose to meet his attacker. They encountered, and the wolverine flung the puppy back. Seconds later the wolverine was staring about in bewilderment. The puppy had vanished, and it took him some time to realize what had happened.

Where there had been a foot-wide gap in the ice bridging the stream, there was now a circular break. Thrown backward by the greater weight of the wolverine, Veddge had crashed through the ice into the water below.

Whining in its disappointment, the hungry hunter padded up and down the stream sniffing and snarling, but there was neither sound, sight, nor smell of what he had hoped would be a good meal.

Veddge hardly knew what had happened to him. One second he was face to face with the wolverine. The next, he was thrown backward and did not even hear the tinkling crack of breaking ice as he went through to the swiftly running water below.

The shock of the icy cold took his breath, and for perhaps ten seconds he could do no more than gasp and struggle to keep his head above water. Before he finally gathered his wits and got to his feet, he had been carried a hundred yards or more downstream.

Above him a foot-wide strip of blue sky was showing through the gap in the ice. After scrabbling with his strong left paw, he managed to break a larger gap and climb through the ice.

Shivering, he shook the freezing water from his coat, then began to limp south, away from the spot where he had so nearly met his death. He continued to shake himself until finally his coat was dry.

The silence was broken by the lonely *peee-eeee-eeee-eeeeep* of a golden plover. Its thin call sounded like the squeaking of a rusty gate hinge. The bird was not far away, beautiful against the dazzling white of the sunlit snow, but Veddge was not interested in beauty. He was hungry, and even a mouthful of food would be welcome.

Keeping as close to the snow as possible, he inched his way nearer; but he was hampered by his lame right forefoot. The plover continued to call, hoping to attract a mate, but it still kept a watchful eye on the approaching puppy.

When Veddge was about ten yards from the golden plover, it winged easily into the air and flew to a dwarf birch some distance away. There it continued to call, making the only sound in that vast and lonely space. Veddge realized it was no use trying again, and he sat staring longingly at the bird.

Finally, he turned and limped away, seeking the shelter of a cluster of dwarf birch trees. There he lay through the remainder of the short day, licking the braid bandage on his damaged leg. He was hoping something would come—a Lapp, or a dog, even a few reindeer. Anything alive would give him hope that he would soon be found and taken back to Aslak.

No one came. The calling of the golden plover grew fainter as the bird moved away. The lemon-colored sun sank toward the horizon, and the water which had been dripping all day from the birch twigs froze and turned to icicles with the approach of evening.

Veddge was hungrier than he had ever been. He spent a miserable night under the birch trees. When he finally drifted off into an uneasy sleep, he dreamed of juicy reindeer bones or bowls of the thick porridgy mush that the Lapps feed to their dogs.

Veddge was wakened once. The night was alive with the howl of a wolf. The hairs on Veddge's shoulder and neck were stiff with fear, and every muscle became taut. Like the wolverine, the wolves had not had an easy winter. They were all lean and hungry, and if they had caught Veddge's scent, they would have tracked him down and finished him off in minutes. The puppy sat taut muscled until the wild calls died away and the night was silent again.

He had drifted off to sleep again when the darkness to the north suddenly waned. A white glow spread across the far horizon, as though a distant town was lighting up. Then banners of light, like searchlight beams, began to shine across the sky. Some were white, others were pale green, pink, and blue. They brightened until they lit up the snow and transformed the birch trees into strange dreamlike objects.

§ 33

The lights woke Veddge from his doze and he stared upward. Where there were lights there was usually a man. Where there was a man there would be food!

Hopefully he stared about, but there was no movement, no sound—nothing to suggest man, or reindeer, or the warmth of a Lapp tent. Then suddenly out of the empty night came a big bird. With noiseless wings beating the cold air and its eyes like two small yellow moons, an Arctic owl came down with no more noise than a falling snowflake.

There seemed to be no reason for the owl to swoop like this, yet when its feet were about six inches from the snow, the large talons opened. When they closed, there was a tiny squeak and a momentary flurry of movement from something the owl had picked up.

The big wings started to beat quicker, and after hovering for a second only inches from the snow, the owl began to lift upward into the air again. At that moment Veddge forgot his lame leg. His eyes were blazing with sudden hope as he launched himself in a desperate leap, hoping to knock the bird out of the air. It was a hopeless leap. Its down-covered wings fanning the air with tremendous power, the owl rose easily out of reach of the puppy's paws. Yet the leap was not entirely without reward. Startled by the unexpected appearance of the puppy, the owl momentarily opened its claws. As a result, the little furry creature it had killed dropped almost at Veddge's feet.

For a moment the young puppy waited, half expecting the thing to run for its life. When it did not move, he sniffed,

and the smell made him realize more than ever how hungry he was. When he had finished eating, he felt a little better, though he was still hungry.

It was then that Veddge began learning how to hunt for his own food. As he sniffed about, he got a faint, warm smell. It was a good smell—the smell of food—and he nosed nearer the snow-covered grass. The grass was dead and stiffened by the frost. It tickled his nose and made him sneeze.

Strangely enough, it was the sneeze that told him there might be more food quite close to him, for after the sneeze, there was the faintest of squeaks from the dead grass and a rustling as if something tiny had moved. No human ear could have picked up the sound, but Veddge heard it. There was something living in that tangle of snow-covered dead grass.

Veddge's eyes blazed with sudden excitement. That faint rustle had been made by tiny scampering feet. In his excitement he forgot his injured leg and leaped, both paws spread wide. A second later he uttered a howl of pain as his injured leg was badly jarred, sending a pang of agony up to his shoulders.

Whimpering with pain, he slumped down and licked the bandaged leg until the pain died down. Yet even as he licked, his ears were cocked and he was listening. He was hoping to hear again that faint whispering; but there was no sound. After a long wait he thrust his nose into the dead grass, sniffing hopefully. He was disappointed. The warm, appetizing smell was no longer there.

Whatever had been in the grass had left, perhaps frightened by the puppy's sneeze or by the owl which had swooped so silently and attacked one of the little creatures.

The northern lights began to fade. Their long streamers grew smaller and drew back to the polar north like a retreating army. Soon there was only the twinkle of stars to show that the clouds had now vanished completely, leaving a clear, cold sky.

Still desperately hungry, Veddge inched his way to the tiny bank where dead grass tips pushed through the snow like fine black needles. Hopefully he sniffed until his nose was pushing through the top crust of snow. He continued to sniff and was finally rewarded by picking up a very faint scent of some warm living thing. It gave him fresh hope, and he lay there with ears cocked, sniffing deep and waiting. Then he heard the faintest of squeaks. Something was coming!

He moved his right paw sideways so that it could rest easily and be out of the way. Then, as the faint squeaking came again, he began digging with the blunt claws of his left paw. Immediately the squeaking stopped. There was a soft rustling sound, and again the lemmings had scurried deeper into the grass, completely out of reach.

Refusing to give up, Veddge dug for ten minutes and uncovered a network of tiny runways more than a yard long. The smell of life was stronger, but there was no other reward. The lemmings had vanished, and Veddge was still hungry.

Disappointed and tired, he lay and licked the padding

§ 37

about his injured leg and tried to forget his hunger. He made no noise at all—and it was this silence that got him a meal.

After a while, half dozing, he again heard the squeaking. His ears pricked up at once and his eyes opened. He made no attempt to reach the dark patch where his digging had disturbed the snow and laid the ground bare. Hunger was teaching Veddge the first rule of hunting—absolute stillness and perfect quiet.

His nostrils began to twitch when he got the warm scent of the lemmings, and his muscles tightened. He knew they were very near, though he could see no movement at all. To get one he must lie so still that they would come out into the open, come out close enough for him to be able to snap one up before it could get away.

Without warning, the Arctic owl reappeared. It had been floating above on silent wings. Its eyes could see many things Veddge could not see, and its ears were even keener than those of the dog. The owl had heard the faint squeaks as the lemmings came to see what had happened to their covered runways.

Soundless as a falling feather, the bird dropped out of the sky. Its talons were stretched to their full extent so that they were like great curved hooks. Once in their clutch, no small creature could survive.

Too late the squeaks stopped. Too late the half dozen lemmings tried to rush back into the shelter of their grass tunnels. As the owl's talons closed over a plump body, there was a thin squeak of terror. The squeak was cut short as the lemming's life came to a sudden end. Then the big wings were beating again as the killer started to lift itself and its victim into the air.

At that moment Veddge came to swift life. The muscles in his back legs swept him off the snow and into the air. In the same instant his undamaged paw was striking out. It was a wild, sweeping blow, but luck was with him. He hardly seemed to touch anything; yet he had struck the owl's right wing. The bird was thrown off balance and brought to the ground in a flutter of feathers.

There was a short, sharp scream of pain and anger. Veddge yelped as something that felt like a red-hot dagger dug into the side of his nose. It was the hooked beak; but it was the last blow the Arctic owl struck, for a moment later Veddge had made his first kill.

Hunt or die!

Holding down the dead owl with his left paw, Veddge squatted in the snow and curled his tongue round his nose to lick the place where the hooked beak had struck him. It was a painful gash, and he would carry the scar to the day he died; but it was a small price to pay for a meal. The owl was a large bird, large enough to satisfy Veddge's hunger.

It was the first time Veddge had tried to eat a bird, and he did not find it easy. The tiny, downy breast feathers got into his nose and tickled so much that he sneezed and sneezed. He laid the owl down and took the edge off his appetite by eating the lemming. It was no more than a good mouthful, but it made him feel better. When he had finished it, he tackled the owl with greater care, soon learning how to deal with the bird.

With the new day came sunshine and even a suggestion of warmth. Where Veddge had made his first kill there was an untidy scattering of feathers, all that was left of the Arctic owl. Just in case he had missed a morsel of food, Veddge scattered the feathers, then limped across the softening snow to a little stream, where he drank his fill. One or two small, fleecy clouds drifted slowly across a pale blue sky. It was a day holding the promise of spring—a day to mark the real end of another long, hard winter.

Throughout Lapland the reindeer would be moving northward. The calves were always born as far north as possible, for when the sun melted the snows, the mosquitoes appeared. Hatching out in their millions by the side of every bog or lake, the winged pests could make life unbearable for the reindeer; thus the herds moved north.

Though Veddge did not realize it, he had been left in a kind of summer no-man's-land. The Lapps had taken their reindeer northwest for the summer months, and hardly a human being would come here. Only the wild life and the mosquitoes were left. For at least four months he would not see a single man, woman, or child.

Throughout the remainder of that day, the puppy lay quietly dozing or licking his aching foreleg. The meal of one lemming and one very tough, stringy Arctic owl had driven back the pangs of hunger.

Once he thought he heard the distant calling of a Lapp herdsman, a faint *aw-aw-aw-awawawaw!* Quivering with excitement and hope, he scrambled up on his three strong legs, his ears pricked, his eyes blazing with hope. He barked and barked, then listened intently. If there was a herdsman nearby, he did not answer the puppy's frantic yelps. Gradually the excitement died from Veddge's eyes and he lay down again.

Though there was still a lot of snow about, it was melting, and the sun was setting later and later each evening. Soon it would not set at all, but swing low on the horizon at midnight for an hour, then begin to rise for the new day. This was the land of the midnight sun. For Veddge it had become the land of hunger.

He limped back to the spot where he had caught the owl the previous night. The sun had set, and the light was beginning to fade again. He could see the scattered feathers and the black scar on the little bank where he had dug into the runways of the lemmings. He lay as close to the earth as he could, his ears pricked, listening for the first faint squeaks that would tell him the tiny creatures were coming within his reach.

As he lay waiting, he heard through the still, frosty air a faraway howling; the sound sent a shiver through Veddge. Though he did not know it, this was a bad time of the year for wolves. They had gone through a hard winter and were lean from hunger. They came out on the uplands in the hope of snatching a weakly reindeer or an early-born calf.

Veddge's eyes glowed brilliant green, and he hugged the damp earth closely. He had already forgotten his lucky escape from the wolverine, but he did not want to meet even one wolf.

Hungry, he dozed throughout the night, awakening as morning came to the sound of blackcock. To attract the hens, the cocks were already displaying their plumage, tails arched over their backs, beaks thrust forward as they dared other cocks to come near. Their sharp cries, *shiooeee*

—shiooeee—shioeee! rang out in the cold, clear air of early morning.

Veddge's eyes were alight with sudden interest as he slowly got to his feet. He had caught one bird; he might catch another. He made his way cautiously toward the sounds. The blackcock were in a small clearing, ringed by dwarf birch trees. Even if the presence of the blackcock had not been a sign of approaching spring, the birch trees told of its coming. Despite the snow of two nights earlier, the buds were fat and ready for bursting. Spring was coming —and coming quickly.

Veddge was not interested in spring or its beauties; he wanted food. Crouching as close to the earth as possible, he got to the very edge of the birch trees. Watched by several hens, two blackcock were challenging each other. Their tails were arched up almost over their backs. Their heads were thrown back, and they were prancing about, each waiting for the other to make a move.

Suddenly they came together, leaping a foot into the air, their beaks jabbing and feathers flying. It seemed the right moment for Veddge to grab a juicy mouthful, and he started to run. The instant he put his right paw down, however, it hurt, and the pain brought a startled yelp from him.

The blackcock forgot their fight. With a frantic fluttering of wings, cocks and hens flew a hundred yards away to perch in the highest tree. Sadly Veddge watched them for a minute and then turned and limped away.

For the next two days he did not taste any food at all.

Hunger took the gloss from his coat and his ribs began to show. There *was* food for those clever enough to get it, for ducks by the hundreds were coming north to mate and bring up their families. This was a land of lakes, large and small, and each day the water grew noisier with the quacking of ducks and the whirring of wings.

Time after time Veddge stole cautiously to the edge of a lake and peered through the reeds now springing up through the rotting ones of the previous year. Ducks were everywhere, and a few large geese. They were feeding, dibbling in the mud, or preening their glossy feathers. They all looked happy and well fed.

Sometimes ducks would come quite close to the reeds while Veddge stood like a statue, panting with excitement at the thought of a meal. The moment he made a move, however, there would be a sudden splash-splash-splash, a beating of sturdy wings, and the ducks would be gone.

Veddge grew hungrier and leaner until the evening of the third day, when he saw a fox. She was a vixen and looked as lean and hungry as the puppy. She had more than herself to think of, for she had a litter of seven young cubs to feed, and she taught Veddge a lesson on how to hunt.

As the vixen drew close to the lake, at a point where there were no reeds, the ducks swimming nearby stopped their feeding. They were ready to scurry away if this lean-looking hunter stepped into the shallows. The vixen hardly seemed to notice the ducks. She lapped a little water, then drew back.

Veddge was interested, but he knew he could not hope to catch the vixen. His injured leg was not quite as painful now, but he still limped. He lay down and watched in amazement, for the vixen had begun a queer kind of dance. At the water's edge she pranced on her hind legs, jumped this way and that, and even spun round as if trying to catch her own tail. It was all done in complete silence, without even a glance at the ducks.

After a few minutes several ducks began to swim nearer the edge of the lake. They were like spectators anxious not to miss anything of this strange show. Others followed when it seemed there was no danger. If the fox saw them, she gave no sign but kept leaping this way and that, then standing on her hind legs, or whirling about as if anxious to snatch at the tip of her tail.

Veddge's eyes narrowed as the ducks gradually drew nearer and nearer the land. His mouth began to water at the thought of what he could do if ducks came so close to him. His muscles tightened and slowly he raised himself erect.

Just as he was beginning to steel himself for a rush into the water, the vixen ended her playing. In the middle of a swiveling dance when she seemed intent only on catching the tip of her own tail, she leaped out into the shallows.

In an instant there was a tremendous flurry of wings, and the air was filled with a frightened quacking as the ducks flung themselves upward. One did not get away, and a few moments later the triumphant vixen splashed ashore with a dead duck held firmly in her jaws.

Veddge came to life then. With a threatening bark he

began a swift but limping run toward the fox. The vixen, muddied to the shoulders, turned in surprise. For a moment she stared at the advancing puppy, but realizing he was too big for her, she raced away with her prize at a speed Veddge could not hope to match.

Veddge watched her go, then turned back sadly to the water's edge. So much food, so near, and yet not a mouthful for him! Overhead a crowd of angry birds, shovelers, teal, mallard, and even some stately swans, were flying around, alarmed by what had happened. They would keep a wary eye on the puppy, and any hope of his doing what the cunning vixen had done was out of the question.

Splashing into the shallows, he lowered his head to drink and almost poked his nose into a nest containing eleven eggs! He had never eaten an egg, but after cautiously crunching one, drawing back in alarm as the eggshell crackled in his jaws, he began to eat, and when he finished, there was nothing left but broken eggshells.

Filled with hope of finding more food, he began to search among the reeds, but within a minute there was an interruption. With a tremendous beating of wings two big geese came down. They flew so close to him that he felt the downdraft from their passing. The gander settled on the water and with a tremendous hissing drove Veddge out of the shallows.

He returned twice that day when the ducks seemed to have settled down again, but each time there was such an uproar that he was forced to retreat. Later, he hobbled across to another lake about half a mile away, and there he

§ 46

had another success. He found a nest with four eggs and again left nothing but crunched-up shells.

For ten days after that, Veddge lived on eggs. His leg began to improve, and the swelling went down so much that eventually he was able to walk on four legs. To run was painful, though, and he had a slight limp.

On the eleventh day, when the sun was setting only for an hour, he found a lake with a dense thicket of stunted trees growing along the eastern shore. As at the other lakes, the water was alive with ducks, even two graceful swans. Their nest was plain for all to see. It was an untidy "island" in the reeds, and Veddge made straight for it. There were eggs in the nest, for one bird was sitting and the other keeping guard.

As he splashed through the shallows Veddge heard a warning hiss from the cob (male swan). Stopping, with his right forepaw raised, Veddge snarled a warning. Hunger had made him bold, and he was learning quickly that if he was not to grow weaker and weaker, he must have meat. Eggs were not enough.

The hissing increased until it sounded like steam from a leaky pipe. The cob was warning him not to come any nearer. Veddge barked again. A powerful and angry father swan faced the half-grown and very hungry dog. They remained motionless for perhaps twenty seconds, neither moving, neither making a sound.

From the nest came a warning hiss, and the pen (mother swan) stepped out of the clutter of twigs and reeds with which the nest had been built. She did not

wait for Veddge to bark. Long neck thrust out, her power-ful wings beating the air, she launched herself at the in-truder. As if he had been waiting for this, the father swan also charged. His wings were so strong that a blow from one could break a man's arm. The previous year these two had had to defend their nest against a lone wolf. The wolf was old, but desperately hungry, and he was big. Yet the swans had managed to batter him until he had fallen flat in the slime. Then a powerfully jabbed beak had driven into his neck, and he had died. In defense of their nest the two swans were absolutely fearless.

Veddge had never met swans before, but he turned to run when the mother swan charged. His limping foreleg betrayed him, and he slipped. A wing knuckle just grazed his head, but the blow was sufficient to daze him and send him flopping into the slime.

As he had done with the wolf, the father swan jabbed with his murderously powerful beak. The blow was aimed at the back of the puppy's neck, and even if Veddge had known what was coming, he could not have dodged, for he was still trying to get his head out of the choking slime. For him, Death was in the air.

Wilderness ways

The mother swan saved Veddge. Her fury was such that she hardly realized her mate was coming in to deliver the final blow. She beat at the fallen puppy with her right wing, and the blow took the male swan hard on the shoulder. It turned him sideways, and the orange beak splashed harmlessly into the mud.

To keep his balance the male swan spread his wings, and for seconds both swans were off balance as their wings interlocked. In those few seconds Veddge got his head out of the slime, and though still dazed, he began to stagger away.

Both swans made as if to follow him, but he slithered into a thick growth of young rushes. There he turned, snarling defiantly as the first swan tried to get at him. The mother swan jabbed her orange-colored beak through the reeds, and Veddge snapped at it. For a second his teeth closed over the tip, and he hung on.

The swan gave a strangled hiss and tried to draw back, but Veddge hung on with all his strength. Now his head was beginning to clear, and he released his grip on the beak only when the other swan came round to try to dislodge him. The battle lasted several more minutes, and there was trouble for both sides.

Veddge received several painful jabs on the shoulders, but in return he drew blood from the male swan, and he had broken the tip of the mother swan's beak. Hissing and flapping their wings, the two big birds splashed around the thick tussock in which Veddge was hiding, but he kept them at bay. Finally, the mother swan went back to the nest, leaving her mate to watch the imprisoned puppy.

The little lake grew quiet again as the disturbed ducks returned to their feeding. Twice the father swan pretended to give up the battle, only to return with a flurry of wings when Veddge made as if to leave his refuge. After that, the angry swan paddled into deeper water and began to preen his feathers.

Sore and bleeding from two jabs on the shoulders, Veddge slunk back to land. He was covered in slime from head to foot and still hungry, but he did not stop until he was far away from that lake. There were some lessons a young dog in the wilderness had to pay dearly to learn, and one of these was not to try to dine off swans' eggs.

He washed himself in a stream flowing out of one lake and into another at a lower level, and there he had a piece of much-needed luck. As he lay by the side of the stream, licking his wounds and his bruises, he saw a silvery splash in the shallows. Raising his head, he stared, suddenly alert. All his thoughts were on food, and as the silver splashed again and again, he paddled into the water.

There was no reckless rush this time. The fish looked like an easy prize, but Veddge had no wish to run into danger again. He watched for a minute while the fish, which had allowed itself to be carried from the upper lake and which was now in water too shallow for easy swimming, struggled to get over the stones. It was indeed a prize, for it was fat and in weight must have tipped the scales around four pounds. Veddge finally plucked up courage to snatch at the struggling shiny thing. He was panting with eagerness as he carried it through the shallow water to the bank and lay down to eat.

From that time Veddge ceased to be hungry. The stream proved to be a continuous source of food. The snow which melted on the higher fells in the long summer days rushed down into the upper lakes. From there the water passed down shallow streams to lower lakes, and it was in the shallows of these streams that Veddge found his food.

For hours each day he sat on the banks of one stream or another, watching the flashing water for a sign of a struggling fish. Sometimes they were small, often they were quite large, for no one ever fished these lakes. By the time midsummer came, his wounds and his bruises healed, and even his foreleg ceased to trouble him, though he would walk with a slight limp to the end of his days.

Quickly he changed from the raw puppy of earlier days. His coat grew sleek, his ribs ceased to show along his flanks, and there was an alertness in his eyes and in the way he walked like that of a young wolf.

Until the day he stumbled on a hare, he had almost

forgotten the taste of meat. He was running out of sheer joy when he stepped onto the hare lying hidden in the tussock of grass. As the hare began to rise, Veddge snapped. In this desolate country a hunter had to be either very quick or very clever.

Veddge had learned to be both. Having tasted meat once again, he decided to go back to where the lemmings lived for a change of diet. The little furry creatures were not easy to catch. They loved to play out in the sunshine for an hour or so each day, but they were careful. Like rabbits in other countries, they were never far from an escape hole.

Several days Veddge went to hunt them and failed. Then he learned that patience was the answer. He lay on the bank top, immovable and quiet, waiting. His hearing had grown sharper than ever; but even when he heard the first faint squeaks as the lemmings began to poke their noses through the wiry grass, he did not move. Only when they had been scampering about, unaware that he was watching them, did he pounce. He became quick enough to catch two at a time.

Life was good, and Veddge was happy. He was not aware of the passing of time. For some weeks the sun never set. It would sink close to the northern horizon, then seem to slide along for an hour before beginning to rise again for the new day.

In those weeks of almost endless daylight, Veddge grew amazingly. Though he had been born only at the end of the previous summer, the hard life he now lived toughened him even more than if he had been herding the reindeer. As the weeks passed he lost all sign of his earlier puppy days.

He continued to fish and to hunt for lemmings until one day he noticed there was less water flowing from lake to lake. The snow on the fell tops was no longer melting, so less and less water was flowing into the upper lakes.

There was a nip in the air. Fish were harder to catch, and even the lemmings were spending less time in the open. As a result, he caught fewer of them. He had to spend more time fishing, but those fish he caught were smaller than usual. Life suddenly became much harder.

The days shortened. Now Veddge had to prowl throughout the whole day. He became expert at catching voles as well as lemmings. He learned to wade almost shoulder deep into the lakes for his fish. Finally, the day came when there was a sudden fall in the temperature, and he awoke to find the reeds by the lakeside white with frost and a coating of ice over the lake.

Food became scarcer and scarcer, for the lake and even the stream froze over. After the first snowfall, the only living things were the ptarmigan and the owls. The blackcock had gone, many of them traveling across Finland and southern Sweden to the North Sea, and across that to the moorlands of Scotland. Only the ptarmigan remained, and it took Veddge several days before he learned how to catch these big birds.

The ptarmigan burrowed into the snow to peck at the reindeer moss on which they fed. A small hole in the snow did not necessarily mean that a ptarmigan was directly beneath. They seemed able to move about at ground level, for the snow was soft.

Veddge lay in the first snow of winter for three hours near a small wood of stunted birch trees. There were ptarmigan in the wood, for he had heard them calling. At last, four flew down to the snow, vanishing in a sudden burst of white spray as they burrowed below the surface to where they could feed.

Half afraid they might burst out of the snow before he got to them, Veddge trotted across, sinking belly deep in the soft whiteness. As he drew near the first small depression in the snow, the thing he feared happened. With a sudden wild flapping of wings and a startled *kopek— kopek-kopek-pek-pek-pek!* one of the big birds burst out of the snow and flew like a rocket back to the trees.

Throwing caution to the winds, Veddge raced across to the next hole and was lucky, for the ptarmigan beneath had been burrowing toward him. It was pecking ravenously until faintly through the snow it heard the alarm call of the one that had escaped.

Up through the snow came the big cock—right into Veddge's jaws. He fed well, for the bird was still plump after easy autumn pickings of ground berries. Yet even a prize like this was not enough, and the ptarmigan would be much harder to catch in the future. The days were shortening so quickly now that the birds could afford to wait until dusk cloaked their flight down to their feeding places.

Veddge caught only four birds in a week and was

growing thinner when one night, as the last hint of daylight faded in the west, he heard a sound that sent a thrill of delight through him. The sound was far away, and only ears as keen as his had become would have picked it up. It was a faint *aw-aw-aw-awawawaw!*—the cry of a Lapp reindeer herder to his dogs. The unseen man was commanding them to circle the herd and bring them closer to him.

The call reminded Veddge of all the things he had known in the first few months of his life—the cheerful voice of Aslak; the family tent with its smoky fire and the smell of reindeer meat cooking; the porridgy food he got and the occasional scrap of steaming reindeer meat tossed to him as he crouched by the tent door.

Veddge did not hesitate. He pointed his nose toward the sound and began to run. Twice he had to stop to chew at hard pads of snow which formed on his paws, but the moment the pads had been removed, he went on. Over a ridge, down through a long wood of small trees whose leaves had already been scattered by the first harsh blasts of approaching winter, and on to a valley where he got his first scent of woodsmoke. He knew that smell; slightly acrid, but reminding him so clearly again of the things he had known in his earliest days. His eyes were blazing with eagerness as he ran. *He was going home!*

A hundred yards out of the wood the smell of burning birch was even stronger. Had he known where to look, he would have seen a procession of sparks swirling up through the gap in the top of the Lapp tent; but the smell of woodsmoke was sufficient for him.

He was whimpering in his eagerness to get back to Aslak and the others until, without warning, the quiet of the night was shattered. A brilliant flash of orange fire dazzled his eyes while the roar of a shotgun right ahead was like thunder in his ears. Almost at the same moment heavy lead shot droned through the night air like a crowd of homing bees.

Somewhere ahead there was a sharp yelp of pain. While Veddge was still dazzled by the flash and bemused by the thundering roar of the gun, a terrified reindeer stag came charging toward him. Sill some yards away, the stag was brought crashing down as a gaunt he-wolf leaped at its throat.

Veddge slithered abruptly to a stop. He was panting noisily for he had run hard. His nose told him that the animals snarling at the throat of the dying stag were wolves. His nose also told him that the animal they were killing was a reindeer.

In the second or so as Veddge slithered to a sudden stop, these sensations went through his brain. From the time he was a small puppy, he had been trained to defend the reindeer. The skin of a dead wolf had been pushed under his nose, making his eyes burn with green flame. When the scent of that dead skin had made the hair rise on Veddge's shoulders, Aslak had patted him on the back. In this way Veddge had been taught to hate wolves.

There had been other lessons to drive home the fact that wolves were enemies. He remembered these things now and with a snarl of anger charged in toward the pack.

There were seven wolves, the old he-wolf, a she-wolf, and five younger ones.

Only during a time of desperate hunger will wolves attack man, and they associate dogs with men. One of the five younger wolves had been badly stung by several lead pellets from the Lapp herdsman's gun. He was whining in fear and pain, and his fear spread to the others when Veddge came charging in.

Snarling, the pack leaped away from the dying stag, their eyes glowing green. They formed a half circle as the young puppy reached the stag. He stood with one paw on the fallen animal's hindquarters and defied the wolves to return. At that moment he feared nothing. This was his work, defending his master's reindeer.

There were other sounds now coming nearer: dogs barking and a man yelling angrily. Then the darkness was cut by something neither Veddge nor the wolves had seen before. It was a thin but brilliant beam of light. (The Lapp had been tempted into buying a powerful electric torch during a visit to the Norwegian port of Hammerfest. It was this strange new thing that now lit up the scene.)

The herdsman had been delighted with his new *toy*, but now he found it very helpful in the thick darkness of this wintry night. The torch beam flashed over the scene, revealing the wolves and showing Veddge standing on the dying reindeer stag.

The Lapp's dogs were charging in, but their owner bawled an angry command for them to stop. A moment later he leveled his gun and fired a second time.

§ 58

Something more savage than the biggest mosquito bit at Veddge's right ear. It was a pellet from the Lapp's gun. Other pellets stung the wolves. Startled also by the sound and the flash, they turned and ran.

Veddge gave a yelp at the sting of his perforated ear, but when the wolves fled as the herdsman's dogs came racing, Veddge turned and chased after the wolves. He would never have caught them, for his limp cut down his speed, and it was his limp that allowed the three dogs to catch up with him.

Veddge never expected the dogs to attack him. His one aim was to catch the wolves, and he gave a bark of dismay and anger when the nearest dog caught up with him and tried to get a throat hold. Had he succeeded, he would have held Veddge down until the other dogs would have come to help finish him off.

By this time the Lapp herdsman had reached the dying reindeer stag, and the moment he realized what had happened, he made the night ring with his yells of encouragement. If the dogs could kill even one wolf, it would be some satisfaction for his loss, for he could sell the wolf skin.

Veddge rolled over as the first dog tried for a throat grip. He snapped back and limped clear, just as the other dogs arrived. They hurled themselves into the fight. They were trained to kill, whether the enemy was wolf, wolverine, or even the occasional bear. They knew this enemy was not a wolf, but he did not have the usual smell of dog. He had lived too long alone, killing for his food, and that gives an animal its own peculiar smell. Fighting as a team the three dogs tackled Veddge, snapping and snarling and seeking a death hold.

Veddge—the outcast

The months of hunting alone had changed Veddge a great deal. Even an experienced herd dog would have been no match for him. Hunger had taught him to leap and snap with terrifying speed. Those who were not quick did not eat. Even catching the fish as they flopped about in the swift-running shallows had not been easy. The lessons he had learned while he had been alone saved his life now.

As the three dogs rolled him over, he slashed at the nearest. It was a quick, savage bite that made the surprised dog howl and leap away. An instant later Veddge's teeth met in the paw of the second dog. That dog, already feeling for a grip on Veddge's neck, rolled away yelping.

The third dog had managed to get a slight grip on the fur about Veddge's throat and was feeling for a deadlier grip. A quick, hard shake broke the hold, leaving the dog with a mouthful of hair—and Veddge was free.

The dogs would have come in again, but from the darkness came a bellowed "Back . . . BACK . . . B A C K" from the herdsman. Now he had managed to reload his gun, and with his electric torch switched on, he was ready to put the "wolf"—as he thought Veddge was—down for good.

The dogs obeyed, and because Veddge still remembered the commands of his own master, Aslak, he too rushed toward the man. It was unexpected. The herdsman was sure the "wolf" would flee, and before he could lower the muzzle of his gun, Veddge was tearing toward him.

Bang! The gun spat a yard-long orange flame. Veddge yelped. Not a single lead pellet hit him, but the thunderous roar and the sudden leaping tongue of fire gave him a fright. He swerved to one side, running as fast as his slightly lame foreleg would allow him.

Bang! The gun roared a second time, but now Veddge was lost in the gloom, and behind him the dogs were snarling in pursuit. Five minutes later the night was silent again. The Lapp had called his dogs back, and Veddge, his heart thumping wildly, was struggling to regain his breath.

He was puzzled and frightened. From the moment he had first heard the Lapp's long-drawn-out call to his dogs —the familiar *aw-aw-aw-aw-awawaw!*—Veddge's one aim had been to get back to the warm atmosphere of the Lapp tent. He longed for the friendliness of the humans with whom he had lived for the first months of his life.

For several hours after the encounter, he sat staring toward the valley bottom. The night wind kept bringing him whiffs of woodsmoke, and each time he got the smell of burning birch, he whimpered sadly.

Finally, midway through the night he decided to try once more to find his master. He did not know there might be other Lapp families in this lonely country. To him, the smell of man meant Aslak and the others of his family. Using his nose to guide him, he trotted down the gentle slope toward the place where the Lapp tent and the *pulkkas* were as yet unseen in the darkness.

Reaching the spot where the reindeer stag had been killed by the wolves, he paused and sniffed the trampled snow. There was nothing but a vague smell of death. The herdsman had left his dogs to guard the stag while he had gone back for a small *pulkka*.

Quickly and expertly he had skinned the dead animal, then cut it up with the skill of a butcher. The meat would go into the cooking pot; the skin would be cured, and his wife would make clothing from it. There were no antlers, for the stags shed their antlers toward the end of autumn.

Veddge went slowly and cautiously on until he was no more than fifty yards from the little camp. He could make out the conical shape of the tent; could see the occasional spark which floated up through the hole in the top. The smell of burning birch was much stronger here, reminding him more than ever of his young master, Aslak.

Veddge was eager to return to the company of man; but when he was still twenty yards from the tent, there was a faint scuffling and a dog wriggled under the heavy blanketing of the door. Sleeping with one ear cocked, it had heard something and now stood, testing the wind. From within the tent came the sound of a voice as someone spoke to the dog.

Veddge barked. He was trying to tell the unseen man

that he was here. He had been lost but had come home again. That was what his bark was meant to say. The Lapp's dog behaved as any good Lapp dog will when a stranger is near, whether at night or day. He gave a snarl and came racing forward to challenge Veddge and drive him away.

When Veddge did not turn and run, the herdsman's dog stopped. He was waiting for a word from his master—whether to let this strange dog approach or whether to drive it away. He was snarling deep in his throat, and the man inside the tent grabbed for his gun. He thought the wolves were here again. Ramming a cartridge into the gun breach, he crept out of the tent.

He moved as quietly as he could, but both dogs heard him. Veddge's ears were pricked forward as he waited for the sound of a friendly, welcoming voice. The herdsman's dog, made bold by the fact that his master was behind him, snarled and began to advance. Since his master had made no sound, the dog decided this intruder was an enemy.

Veddge broke the silence. His bark was a desperate attempt to tell the man who he was. He was not a wolf. He was Veddge, the puppy who had been lost. He was eager, so eager, to return home and become a herd dog again.

The reply was swift and frightening. Lone dogs were unknown in Lapland, and suddenly afraid, the herdsman fired into the air above Veddge. He did not wish to injure his own dog, but he did want to frighten away this animal which barked like a dog but might be anything. The long, dark winters make the Lapp herdsman afraid of evil spirits.

§ 65

The blackness was slashed by the flame from the gun muzzle, and a moment later the herdsman's dog closed in on Veddge. In the seconds that followed Veddge behaved like a wolf. He did not meet the attack head on, but slipped sideways, nipping the herd dog on the shoulder and rolling him over in the snow. Had Veddge pounced then, he could have killed; but he turned and ran as the Lapp fired again.

There were no more shots that night, for Veddge went back to the birch trees on the valley side. His tail hung low and his head was drooping as he limped along.

When he reached the shelter of the stunted birch trees, their branches drooping under the weight of half-frozen snow, he turned and looked back. There was nothing to be seen; no glow from a fire. And after a moment he lifted his muzzle to the sky and howled.

As a lost child cries when he thinks he is alone and no one cares for him, so Veddge howled. He had tried desperately to return to the tents of man, but they would not have him. They had set their dogs after him, fired a rifle at him. He seemed to know that he was an outcast. No one wanted him, and he filled the frosty night air with his sorrowful howling.

In the valley the howling began to disturb the reindeer. The does with their young calves got to their feet. The calves huddled close to their mothers. Finally, the stags rose. The Lapp herdsmen, two of them with their well-trained dogs, tried to soothe the animals.

They began to *joik*, which is singing a song they make up on the spur of the moment. They sing in the same way that cowboys used to sing to their cattle to soothe them when coyotes were barking or a thunderstorm threatened.

Above the clack of hoofs as the herd milled around came the pleasant voice of a middle-aged Lapp as he sang:

> *There is nothing here to frighten;*
> *Nun-nun-nuuu --- nun-nun-nuuu!*
> *Soon the sky will start to lighten;*
> *Nun-nun-nuuu --- nun-nun-nuuu!*
>
> *Here beneath the valley snow;*
> *Nun-nun-nuuu --- nun-nun-nuuu!*
> *There is food for stag and doe;*
> *Nun-nun-nuuu --- nun-nun-nuuu!*
>
> *If the wolves should come again;*
> *Nun-nun-nuuu --- nun-nun-nuuu!*
> *Each of them will soon be slain;*
> *Nun-nun-nuuu --- nun-nun-nuuu!*

Almost as if the singing had cast a spell, the distant howling stopped. The herd began to slow down. Heads were still lifted and ears were pricked as does, stags, and even the calves listened, but the night was now quiet. The Lapp went on singing, and his voice soothed the herd until they began to sink down into the snow again, to sleep and wait for the dawn. Peace had come back to the valley; but there was no peace at the edge of the wood where Veddge had been barking.

He had stopped howling when in the darkness he had seen two bright green spots. They were about three inches apart, and they were the eyes of an animal. Veddge forgot his sorrow as he looked quickly round. There were more pairs of green eyes. Seven in all. Seven animals, and they had formed a circle round him. Whichever way he turned, he could see eyes.

It was the same wolf family he had encountered earlier in the night. Then he had helped to drive them off the dying reindeer stag. Now his howling had attracted them, and they were here seeking food. They were even hungrier than Veddge, for whatever they killed they divided, and it takes a lot of food to feed seven hungry hunters.

The wolves made no sound as they padded quietly this way and that. They remembered the scent of Veddge. One of the younger ones had a limp where pellets from the Lapp herdsman's gun had lodged in its lower leg. After a minute or so this young wolf lay down and began to nibble at the aching spots, trying to get at the tiny leaden pellets just below the skin.

Veddge remained completely still for a minute or so. Then he had to turn, for the wolves behind were beginning to move in toward him. Spinning round, he snarled, and the wolves retreated.

From then until the first gray began to show in the sky over the Russian border, Veddge was given not a moment's rest. If he faced north, the wolf to the south began to inch nearer. When he spun round, a wolf from the other side would come in.

The sky began to lighten, and down in the valley a

Lapp was heard calling his dogs. The family had decided not to stay there, and the dogs were yapping at the heels of the stags, forcing them to start trotting south. The does and the calves followed the stags. In an hour the valley would be empty of life.

Up here on the slope the wolves were beginning to grow bolder. With the coming of daylight they could see that Veddge was no larger than they were. He was not large enough to provide a good meal, but they could kill and eat him, and still not lose sight of the reindeer herd. A full-grown stag would provide them with plenty of meat, but Veddge would take the first edge off their hunger.

In some way the wolves seemed to have decided how to tackle the dog, for the he-wolf, a big animal already graying about the muzzle, started to walk toward Veddge, forcing him to turn and prepare to meet an attack. As he turned, he heard a faint siss-siss-siss of paws on snow, and one of the younger wolves came in with a rush.

Veddge spun round, meeting the attacker squarely. There was a harsh clashing of teeth, but no damage was done, for at the very last moment the young wolf turned away. He had done his job well, for as Veddge drove him off, the old he-wolf sprang. There was no turning aside for him. He was hungry and meant to kill this young dog at once.

In trying to turn, Veddge slipped. His lame forepaw gave way under him, and that probably saved his life. The old wolf's jaws snapped shut with a sound like a metal trap closing, but the teeth missed Veddge's throat by six inches.

§ 69

In the next second Veddge showed how living alone had changed him. He could think and act much quicker than any ordinary dog. As the wolf stumbled over him, Veddge lifted his head and got a grip at the base of the wolf's powerful neck.

He did not try to hold on, for he sensed that the rest of the wolf pack was closing in. He bit hard, then leaped away, causing the she-wolf and the five young wolves to halt their rush and even back away.

Now all eyes were on the old wolf. He was the leader, and his family stared at him, wondering why he did nothing. He stood with head slightly bowed as if he was thinking.

The she-wolf whined. She was asking him what was the matter, and why he did not pull this dog down and kill him. There was no answer. The gray-jowled leader of the pack remained motionless though there seemed to be a slight quiver of his body.

For a minute and a half there was no other movement. Veddge was watching and waiting. He was taut muscled. He could not run, for the six wolves were round him in a ring. Then one of the younger wolves sniffed. There was a smell of blood in the air. Their leader was injured— badly injured. He still stood motionless, staring at Veddge; but the bright green glow in his eyes was dimming a little. Finally, he shook his head, and as if he had now decided what to do, he moved toward Veddge.

One of the wolf pack!

Few animals can outrun a hungry wolf pack, and with his lame foreleg Veddge would have been brought down before he had covered a hundred yards. He did not even try to run. As the leader of the pack sprang forward, Veddge leaped.

All the courage and fighting spirit which the Lapps have bred into their herd dogs over many years came to the surface in Veddge at that moment. Wolves were enemies of the reindeer, and though there were seven of them, he did not hesitate.

There were snarls from the rest of the pack as wolf and dog met, then a strange silence. Suddenly the heavier animal's head dropped down. A moment later he was sprawled on the ground with a snarling Veddge standing over him.

It was so unexpected that even Veddge was puzzled. He drew back, snarling and waiting for the others to come in, or for the big he-wolf to rise and renew the fight.

Nothing happened. What Veddge did not know was that when he slashed upward at his enemy, his teeth had

§ 71

met in a vital artery in the wolf's throat. The leader of the pack had been dying from that moment of the attack. Now he was dead, his hunting days were ended, and the pack had lost its leader.

As he stood there, Veddge's eyes were glowing as green as the eyes of the six remaining wolves. He was waiting for an attack which did not come. The she-wolf, mother of the other five, whimpered; and stepping slowly forward, she sniffed at the body on the snow. Then she lifted her graying muzzle toward the sky and howled.

The five younger members of the pack stood silently in a half circle, watching their mother and ignoring Veddge. At last the she-wolf stopped howling, and then, sinking down until she was almost sitting in the snow, she inched her way across to Veddge.

Veddge drew back his lips in a silent warning snarl. He was ready for an attack if it came. The other five members of the wolf family watched and waited in grim silence. The she-wolf reached Veddge, then slowly lifted her head and nipped him gently on the side of the jaw.

Veddge stiffened, and the smell of wolf made his eyes glisten like bright green emeralds in the broadening light of the new day. Though every muscle was tense, he made no move. A change had come over the she-wolf. She was no longer a vicious killer. Slowly she lifted her head when Veddge made no move and again nipped gently at his cheek. When he still made no move, she began to lick his neck and ears.

It was a sign that she was accepting him as the new

leader of the family. Suspicious of her, Veddge began to trot away, and at once the she-wolf followed him. The five members of her family fell in line behind her. Whether he liked it or not, Veddge had been given the place of the old wolf he had killed.

Hunger drove Veddge to one of his previous hunting spots—the place where the lemmings sometimes came out to play. There was no sunshine now to tempt them out. The day was brisk, with the raw cold which often follows the first snow and is a sign that another snowfall will come before very long.

The six wolves squatted down, waiting for their new leader to show them how to find food. In desperation as his hunger grew keener, Veddge clawed at the bank where several months earlier he had broken into the lemmings' runways. The runways had been repaired, and the moment he broke through the inch-thick crust of earth, the warm smell of lemmings brought the wolves to their feet, their eyes glowing.

No lemmings appeared, and though all seven listened intently, there was not even a single squeak to suggest that the little furry creatures were anywhere near.

Then the she-wolf showed that she too knew something about hunting lemmings. She broke into the hard earth of the bank a few yards away, scrabbling with a fury that soon brought results. Even before she had penetrated to the runways beneath, there was a reward.

The inhabitants of the lemming colony had grown fat during the summer, and they had also increased in number until there was scarcely room for them all. Now, at the sound of something digging down to them the little creatures panicked. They scattered throughout their runways, squeaking excitedly.

A number of them scurried along runways which led to the spot where Veddge had already broken through. The leaders, in their rush for safety, tried to stop when they saw the daylight and smelled the cold air, but there was no stopping. Those behind were pushing, trying as hard as they could to get away from the other danger, where the she-wolf was already breaking through to their runways.

One after the other, nine lemmings were pushed out into the broken runways and forced into the open. They were pounced on at once and killed so quickly that they probably never knew what had happened.

Afterward the six wolves and Veddge began to dig in other places, and before the lemmings finally retreated to deeper runways, a score had been taken. Yet they were so small that even three lemmings each did not satisfy the hunger of the hunters.

The she-wolf and her family looked toward their new leader when it became apparent they could not hope to catch any more lemmings that day. Veddge hardly knew what to do, for he had never led a wolf pack before. His own hunger, however, made him turn to the stream where he had caught many fish during the pleasant days of summer.

There was no sweet babble of running water now. The stones among which fish had splashed as they were washed down from one lake to another were locked in ice, and the ice was covered with snow.

Unhappily Veddge scraped away the snow, but the ice beneath felt hard as rock. There would be no meal of fish this day, and Veddge turned to find the six wolves staring at him. They were waiting for him to decide what should be done.

Veddge had no idea what to do. During the months since he had been separated from young Aslak and the Lapp family, he had grown tremendously. He was bigger and stronger and much wiser; but it took far more than strength to find food now that winter was returning to the wilderness. The wolves had learned much from their parents. Veddge had had no one to teach him how to hunt when food was scarce.

One of the young wolves whined and looked anxiously at his mother. The she-wolf stared at Veddge, as if waiting for him to make a move. For a minute or more they stood in silence, and then a large snowflake drifted down. Veddge licked it off the tip of his nose. Other flakes followed. There was no wind, and the large flakes descended in a slow, almost lazy way. That was how snow fell when there was going to be a big snowstorm. Veddge did not know this, but the she-wolf did. She had lived through eight hard winters, and she knew all the signs of snow. If they did not kill something substantial very soon, their ribs would be sticking out before the next snow fell.

When Veddge made no move, the she-wolf suddenly turned and began to trot south. Like the others, she looked ghostly, for snow was sticking to the top of her head, her neck, and her back. Veddge followed her, and the five young wolves fell in behind him, trotting in single file and stepping in the tracks their mother was making.

Heading down the valley they soon came upon signs that told them the reindeer had passed that way. Stags, does, and calves had been cropping the reindeer moss, pawing through the light crust of snow to get to their food. The snow was dusted with fragments of earth, for unlike cattle which crop grass, the reindeer pluck up the moss by the roots, leaving telltale patches of earth on the snow.

The falling snow soon blotted out these signs, and in any case the herd had stopped feeding when the snow began to fall. Instead of wandering slowly along, they had begun to trot, heading for the lower levels where feeding would be easier. At a steady trot they moved between twelve and thirteen miles an hour, a speed they could keep up for hours.

That they had kept up this pace was obvious as hour succeeded hour. With the she-wolf still trotting in pursuit, there was no sign of the herd at all. The lowering snow clouds brought the day to an end very quickly, and by 5 o'clock it was dark.

The wolves were accustomed to running continuously for hours, but Veddge was not. Though his muscles had toughened during the past weeks, they were beginning to tire. He was breathing very hard when, for no apparent reason, the she-wolf stopped in her tracks.

Veddge was glad to flop in the snow, but he rose a

moment later when he realized that not only the she-wolf but also the younger members of the pack were all looking to the right. Their ears were pricked as if keen for some sound.

Lifting his own ears, Veddge listened; but for perhaps twenty seconds he heard nothing save his own harsh breathing and the thud-thud-thud of his laboring heart. Snow was still falling, and the big, soft flakes had coated the wolves and dog alike so that they looked like ghost animals.

Veddge flopped back onto the snow, sure that the she-wolf had been mistaken. Not a murmur of sound broke the deep stillness. He began to nibble at a hard pad of snow that had formed under his left forepaw. A moment later his ears were pricked and he was rising to his feet again.

The sound had come once more—the voice of a man! Because the voice was muffled by the falling snow, it was difficult to tell where the man was, but there was no mistake: it was a man, and he was singing.

The song was not the soothing, often sad *joiking* that a herdsman sings at night to calm the reindeer when they are restless. This was a wild, rollicking melody. It made Veddge draw back his lips in a soundless snarl, and the coarse fur on his neck lifted until every hair was stiff as wire. He had heard Aslak and the two Lapps who herded for old Johan sing many times, but never like this. Instead of being glad to hear a man, Veddge was uneasy, afraid.

The singer was old Johan, grandfather of Aslak. After a stay on the islands off the coast of Norway, the Lapps had started south for the winter grazing grounds. There was every sign of an early winter, and even the reindeer were in a hurry.

At a small settlement where they stopped while Aslak's mother, Susannan, bought supplies of coffee, sugar, and salt, Johan met a boyhood friend. He was also a wealthy reindeer owner. Their meeting started the trouble, for Johan had one weakness—he liked brandy.

Ordering Susannan, Aslak, and the two herdsmen to take his reindeer south, Johan insisted on remaining with his friend. He promised to follow on the next day. Susannan had pleaded with him not to stay, and when he refused, she suggested that Aslak also stay. Then, when he started south, Johan would not be alone. At this, the old man had been indignant and angry.

"Am I a boy that I need someone to look after me?" he demanded. "I know this land as I know my own face. I shall follow you when I am ready!" Nothing either Susannan or Aslak could say would make him change his mind. When his reindeer moved on, he stayed with his friend, and they drank a lot of brandy.

Only when people at the settlement warned them that bad weather would soon be there did Johan and his friend part. Harnessing his big reindeer stag to his *pulkka*, and with two bottles of brandy in the pocket of his *peske* (reindeer-skin robe), the old man started south.

Half drunk when he began his journey, he kept his reindeer stag racing far too long, and finally it had to stop from sheer exhaustion. Johan was not worried. He warmed himself with a long drink from his last bottle, wrapped himself in his robe, and promptly went to sleep.

No thought of danger crossed his mind. He had been driving reindeer through the wild lands of this northern country all his life and was afraid of nothing.

When he woke, he drove his reindeer south again until once more the big stag was so tired that it flopped in the snow and refused to move. Johan emptied his last bottle, and after smoking a pipe, he began to sing. It was his singing that attracted the six wolves and Veddge.

Unseen by Johan, the seven animals drew nearer. The wolves were uneasy, for they were afraid of humans, but hunger drove them on. The scent of the big reindeer stag promised a satisfying meal, and they needed plenty of meat to keep them going through this first heavy snowfall.

The she-wolf whined at Veddge. She was asking him to do something since he was now the leader of the pack. Veddge was uneasy. He was eager to go forward, but not for the same reason as the wolves. They were hungry enough to attack; Veddge wanted to return to his old life with the Lapps. When he had tried earlier to rejoin the Lapps, there had been shots—and he had a hole in one ear where a lead pellet had gone through. That attempt to return to the Lapps had resulted in a savage fight for life. Remembering these things, he just stood and stared.

As the seven animals waited in the falling snow, the singing began to falter. Johan was feeling sleepy again;

and after putting away his pipe, he made himself comfortable in the back of the *pulkka*. With the brandy to warm him, he drifted quickly into a deep sleep.

His reindeer stag was slowly regaining some of its strength when out of the night appeared seven pairs of green lights—the eyes of the wolf pack. They came closer as silently as the falling snow. Half expecting a sudden barking, and perhaps a rush of Lapp herd dogs, they moved very cautiously.

There came a faint scuffling sound as the stag scrambled to its feet. It had got the scent of wolves, and a dog, and its eyes bulged with fear. It turned to look back at the *pulkka*, but Johan was already invisible. His white skin robe was covered with snow, and he looked like part of the *pulkka*.

Spreading out into a circle, the wolves and the dog stared in silence. To find a big reindeer unguarded by either man or dogs seemed too good to be true, and they were suspicious. Veddge was as hungry as his companions, but he reacted differently to the scent of the reindeer. To the wolves it meant food. To Veddge it was a reminder of the days when he was a very young puppy. It brought back memories of Aslak and the Lapp tent; of a fire and the smell of cooking; and his mouth watered at the thought of the bowls of hot porridgy food and the occasional juicy bone.

The wolves began to grow impatient. The she-wolf nipped Veddge on the shoulder. Then one of the younger wolves broke the spell. He gave a whimpering snarl and began to move forward.

The she-wolf looked at Veddge, and when he did not move, she suddenly bounded forward. The others followed her example. Whether their leader acted or not, they were going to feed, and there was no one to protect this reindeer stag.

Wolf—or dog?

Veddge proved then that he was not a wolf. He followed the others, but he broke the silence with a snarling bark. Though the snow was muffling most sounds, that bark sounded like a bugle call. It brought life to the quivering, terrified reindeer stag.

A moment earlier he had been standing there, his eyes bulging with fear. He had been too paralyzed with terror to move as he stared at the circle of luminous green eyes; but the bark broke the spell. He gave a mighty lunge forward, which shook clouds of snow off his neck and back, and then he began to fight for his life.

Johan had often boasted that his stag was the best in the whole of Lapland. The next moment showed it was no idle boast. The stag did not wheel away and try to escape. He knew that with a laden *pulkka* behind him he could not hope to outrun a pack of hungry wolves. Instead of fleeing, he charged.

He had already shed his antlers, but he had other weapons of defense, and he used them now. Up on his hind legs he rose, and a moment later down came his two front

§ 84

hoofs in a stabbing blow that would have meant death or serious injury if they had struck one of the wolves.

One knife-edged hoof barely missed the she-wolf, and she leaped for her life. Veddge and the other five wolves slithered desperately away as the stag lunged again, his cloven hoofs making a queer clacking sound.

With his enemies scattered, the stag lunged forward again and settled down into a steady ten-mile-an-hour trot. The *pulkka* jerked and swayed, and the movement wakened Johan.

The heap on the back of the *pulkka*, which had looked like a pile of snow, suddenly came to life as the old man sat up. He reached for the single rein by which reindeer are guided. As he was about to give it a terrific jerk to bring the stag to a halt, he saw a pair of tiny green lights racing alongside him.

Though his wits were fuddled with the brandy he had drunk, Johan knew at once what those green lights were. In the same instant he realized why the big stag was rushing along at such speed.

Wolves!

Instead of jerking on the single rein, Johan gave a yell of encouragement to the stag. Then he felt for the empty brandy bottle, and with an angry yell he flung it backward to where he could see more glowing green eyes and the vague forms of the pack as they followed him.

There was a yelp of pain from one of the younger wolves as the bottle struck it a glancing blow on the side of the head. The wolves scattered, not knowing what had happened. Only Veddge kept on, and after a momentary hesitation the six wolves followed him.

The stag and the swaying *pulkka* were already lost to sight in the snow-filled darkness, but scent cannot be hidden by darkness. Neither Veddge nor the wolves had any difficulty following the scent of the frightened stag.

For three hundred yards the wolves had a hard task keeping pace with the wildly swaying *pulkka*. They were plunging through soft snow, and here the stag had an advantage, for the hoofs of the reindeer are cloven like those of a cow. In addition, the hoofs spread out, providing a grip on swamp, moss, or snow.

After three hundred yards the pace slackened. Johan had sapped the stag's great strength by his reckless riding during the earlier part of the night, and soon not even fear of the wolves could keep the stag's legs moving. His speed slowed, his flanks were heaving, and the breath came from his wide-flared nostrils in great, gasping puffs.

After four hundred yards, the stag suddenly stopped. His eyes were glassy, and all the fight had seeped out of him. He had given his best; he could do no more.

It is said that strong coffee will sober a drunken man very quickly; but fear sobered old Johan far more quickly than the strongest coffee. During those first minutes while the wolves were chasing him, he realized that he had no weapon other than his sheath knife.

No Lapp goes without a knife at his belt, but even the best knife is little use against a pack of six or seven wolves, especially when they are as starved as these wolves were.

§ 87

While Johan was cursing his own stupidity in not traveling with his daughter and the herd, and trying to think what he could do, Veddge bounded up. Johan yelled, and the puppy swerved aside.

Men who spend four months of every year in the almost complete darkness of northern Lapland grow so accustomed to the blackness that their eyes see better at night than those of most other men. Johan frowned as he stared at the panting Veddge. This was not a wolf! This was a dog!

"I didn't bring a dog with me," he muttered, remembering that his daughter and one of his herdsmen had tried to persuade him to keep one of the dogs as company. He looked at the other shapes now standing with Veddge. *They* were wolves. Six wolves and a dog.

For some reason the thought that a dog was running with a wolf pack sent a shiver of fear through him. The long, dark winters made men ready to believe in evil spirits, and though this fear is dying out now, some superstitions remain. There was, for instance, Stallo, a fearsome spirit which was said to be always on the lookout for people who traveled alone. Stallo turned lonely travelers into stones or solitary birch trees. Could this panting dog be the spirit Stallo?

The old man shook himself, trying to drive away his fear. "No one really believes in Stallo," he snarled, and waving his arms threateningly, he yelled at the dog and the six wolves.

Johan knew wolves were afraid of human beings and of the human voice. He was right, for at his yelling the six wolves backed away. Veddge did not move. His eyes were like little green lamps in the darkness, and he stood his ground. He was not afraid of humans.

At his yelling, the big stag began to stumble forward again. He was a gallant animal and would not die without making a tremendous fight for his life; but he was tired.

The *pulkka* shuddered as it scraped over a stone thrusting up from the snow-covered ground, and Johan had to drop to one knee to avoid being thrown out. The *pulkka* rocked under his weight, and the reindeer stag stopped again. Johan flipped the single rein along the stag's neck, shouting encouragement. He had to keep the big stag on his feet. If he fell, the wolves would be upon him, and the moment they tasted blood—that would be the end.

Johan was completely sober now, trying desperately to think of some way of driving off the wolves. Feeling about in the bottom of the *pulkka* in the hope of finding a weapon, his hands touched an odd-shaped lump. For a moment he could not think what it was.

Picking it up, he remembered. A friend in the settlement where he had stayed had given him a splendid piece of reindeer meat as a parting present. It weighed about seven pounds and would have provided Johan with food for at least two days.

Hurriedly shaking off the piece of sacking in which the reindeer meat was wrapped, he was about to throw it to one side when the *pulkka* came to an abrupt stop. His brave reindeer stag had stumbled and was too weary to keep on his feet. He went down and stayed down.

Veddge yelped excitedly and rushed in. The six wolves followed, and the stag would have died within a minute if Johan had not acted. He was a fool where brandy was concerned, but he had not grown rich by allowing wolves, or any other hunter, to kill his reindeer.

With a bellow of rage he leaped off the *pulkka*, swinging the piece of meat in his right hand. As the wolves and Veddge scattered, Johan tossed the meat after them. He threw it as far as he could in the hope that it would give him a minute or so to try to get the reindeer stag back on his feet.

His angry shouts made the tails of the six wolves curl down between their legs as they scattered. Veddge was running, but he was not as frightened as the wolves. He saw the thing that the old man had thrown, and he got the scent of it—meat, reindeer meat.

Quick as a flash he pounced on the meat and had torn a mouthful from it before the wolves realized what was happening. Snarling, they turned for a share. Within seconds Veddge was fighting to defend his prize. The she-wolf rushed in and almost snatched the meat from Veddge's jaws. Snarling, she pulled viciously, her eyes seeming alight with green fire. The rest of her family padded around, whimpering and trying to pluck up courage to dart in and snatch a mouthful.

None of them did rush in, for though the she-wolf was

their mother, she would have been quick to punish with a slashing bite. When starvation threatened, the food went to the strongest. The weak got what was left when the others had eaten. Whimpering and whining, the five young wolves trotted here and there while the tug-of-war between Veddge and their mother went on.

There could have been only one end to the battle, for the she-wolf was heavier than the dog. Veddge refused to loosen his grip on the meat and was being dragged across the snow. The struggle could not have lasted, for Veddge's teeth were slowly biting through the meat; and when he would have bitten through it, he would have had just a small mouthful, and the she-wolf would have had the rest, the biggest piece.

Johan was hardly aware of the struggle, for after throwing the piece of meat as far as he could, he turned to help his reindeer stag. He knelt by its head and turned it so that the mouth and nostrils were clear of the snow. Then he did what seemed like a very strange thing. He clamped a hand over the stag's nostrils after it had drawn a deep breath. The stag struggled, but for thirty seconds Johan prevented the animal from breathing out.

It seemed like a cruel thing; yet it helped tremendously. Because the stag had to hold its breath in, its heartbeat slowed down from the terrific thump-thump-thump-thump, and that helped drive away some of the panic. Old Johan was said to be the shrewdest reindeer man in the north. He certainly knew what to do when things went wrong.

§ 91

He had just taken his hands off the stag's nostrils when he became aware of the desperate tug-of-war nearby. The she-wolf, all her efforts directed to forcing Veddge to release the lump of reindeer meat, was dragging the dog nearer and nearer to Johan.

At the scuffling and hard breathing, the old man turned. He saw the dim shapes of two animals, one slowly dragging another closer to him. The other wolves were padding about excitedly. They wanted to help their mother but were afraid of the man.

Johan rose. Dragging his heavy knife from its sheath, he gave a terrifying yell and stabbed at the hindquarters of the she-wolf. It was a blow that would have finished her off had the blade struck its target. Startled by Johan's shout, however, the she-wolf had leaped aside, the knife merely slicing a few hairs from her tail. Yet it had helped Veddge, for in jumping to safety, the she-wolf released her grip on the piece of meat. Johan rushed toward the puppy, yelling and waving his knife. Veddge backed away but kept his jaws firmly clamped on the meat.

One of the younger wolves turned his muzzle to the sky and howled. It was the hunger howl, a blood-chilling cry that can make the bravest man shiver. It caused Johan to turn back to his reindeer. If the stag died, his own chance of reaching safety would be very small.

In the past few minutes he had realized he was no longer a young man. Until he had become rich enough to employ men to herd his reindeer, Johan had spent much of his time during the winter months skiing across the snow-covered fells to guard his herd. It had kept him fit and tough. Now, older and without skis to help him cross the deep snow, he would soon tire. If he was to survive, he had to keep his reindeer stag from the wolves. Knife in his right hand he went across and knelt once more at the fallen animal's head.

Veddge, with the meat gripped firmly, was looking for some place where he could eat without being attacked, and the *pulkka* seemed the best possible place. The *pulkka* had a strong man-smell about it, but that did not worry Veddge. He leaped onto the back of the boat-shaped sledge, snarled a warning at the wolves, and began to eat.

The she-wolf's eyes were bright as green lamps as she drew nearer. She had the taste of meat in her mouth but had not even had a mouthful. With her family she came slowly toward the back of the *pulkka*, keeping as far away from Johan as possible.

The snow, which had been falling steadily, had thinned out in the past few minutes and then stopped. The sky above was clearing, and through gaps in the clouds a half moon began to shed a cold light on the scene. The snow turned to silver, and the stunted trees, their branches laden with snow, took on queer, ghostly shapes.

Silent, eyes glowing, the wolves drew slowly nearer. They were very hungry and had to do something quickly if Veddge was not to gulp down every scrap of the reindeer meat.

The she-wolf made the first bold move. She leaped forward but swerved aside as Veddge dropped the meat

§ 93

and made a vicious snap at her. As she drew back, the youngest wolf came in from the other side. He actually leaped onto the *pulkka*, only to be sent rolling off, howling as Veddge nipped one of his ears in a lightning-swift attack. Hunger was making him even bolder than the wolves.

Old Johan helped Veddge, though he did not mean to. Realizing that something was going on at the back of the *pulkka*, he left the reindeer for a moment. Running and at the same time swinging his knife, he yelled at the top of his voice. The wolves scattered at once, but Veddge remained with what was left of the meat between his paws. He bared his teeth at the old man.

Johan hesitated. Had it been a wolf, he might have swung his knife—but this was a *dog*, and the fear that it might be the Stallo spirit stopped him. He swore, then drew back as Veddge continued to stare at him with eyes shining bright in the moonlight.

For a moment or so man and dog remained glaring at one another. Then Johan turned back to his reindeer. The six wolves were standing in a ring about the *pulkka*, afraid of the man. While they stood there, Veddge continued to gulp down meat as fast as he could.

He had learned a lesson while he had been alone in the wilderness, and it was one he would never forget: When there is plenty of food, eat; eat until you cannot eat more.

He swallowed almost six pounds of the reindeer meat before stepping off the back of the *pulkka*, leaving what remained for whichever wolf dared dash in and get it. It was the youngest wolf, whose ear Veddge had nipped so painfully, that dashed in and snatched the meat. Even then the young wolf got no more than a fragment, for his mother, the she-wolf, bowled him over and picked up the meat as he dropped it.

It was the law of the wilderness: food went to the bold and the strong. The she-wolf gulped down the last morsel of meat while her family stood and watched until one lifted his muzzle again toward the moon and began to howl.

The others joined him, and for perhaps two minutes the night was hideous with the blood-chilling howling. The noise made the exhausted reindeer stag lift his head, and he would have struggled to his feet if Johan had not calmed him. The old man did not want the stag to rise until he was rested enough to make another run for life.

Veddge did not howl. He was feeling more satisfied than he had for a long time, and lying down he began to yawn. He would have been quite happy to go to sleep after his heavy meal, but he rose in a minute or so upon realizing that the six wolves were closing in on him.

When the she-wolf had crawled to him two days earlier, her belly scraping the snow, it had been to accept him as the new leader of the pack. That was changed now. He had eaten; they were still hungry. He was *not* a wolf. Now they were ready to kill and eat him.

Veddge sensed this, and the coarse hair on his neck and shoulders bristled until it made him look thicker and more powerful. His legs were stiff; his head was thrust forward; he was ready to fight. He stood and snarled back at the wolves.

The wolves knew that the first to attack this powerful young dog would suffer. He had already shown how quick he was to defend himself. He could not kill them all, but this snarling dog would not die easily. The younger wolves looked to their mother for a lead.

Johan saw what was going to happen, and it gave him new hope. Six wolves were closing in on the strange dog. If they fought, it could only help him. "Go on," he urged. "Go on, fight. I've heard tell that wolves will eat one another if they are hungry enough. I'd help you if I could."

Veddge shot a quick glance at the old man, catching the sound of the muttering. Each time Johan spoke, it reminded Veddge of his puppyhood. In those days the voices of men had meant friendship, food, the warmth of a tent after a long night on the fells. He needed friendship now as he had never needed it before, and he began to back slowly in the direction of the *pulkka*.

Johan swore as the wolves followed. He would have liked them to fight as far away as possible from his *pulkka* and the reindeer stag. He waved his knife, and the moonlight made the blade shimmer like silver. It did not frighten Veddge, who continued to back slowly toward the *pulkka* and the man.

In silence the six wolves closed in. Veddge snarled a warning, but it had no effect. Johan, too, was forced back and moved round the front of his reindeer. As he did so, the stag moved.

Though it had lain so still and silent, the stag could smell the wolves and was quaking with fear. The few

§ 96

minutes rest had slowed down the wild beating of its heart and helped its aching lungs to get much-needed air. In that short time some strength had flowed back into the powerful legs. The snarling of Veddge and the sudden movement of Johan spurred the stag to rise and make a final run for its life.

With a sudden snorting it scrambled to its feet, and the wolves drew back a few paces. Veddge also bounded to one side. Even now he remembered that it had been a reindeer stag that had started all his troubles, leaving him with his limp.

Leaning for a second into the harness of the *pulkka*, the stag gathered its strength and then leaped forward. There was a sharp, cracking sound as the *pulkka* runners, which had frozen into the snow, broke free. Then stag, *pulkka*, and Johan were moving.

The old man hurled himself into the moving *pulkka*, a feat possible only to one brought up on the Lapp highlands. He grabbed the single rein, gave it a slight flick to let the stag know he was with it, then half turned to bellow defiantly at the wolves and the dog.

"Now fight it out among yourselves. You won't get me or my stag."

Old man—young dog!

They were brave words, and within a minute Johan had a feeling he had boasted too soon. The wolf pack took up the chase, but something else equally dangerous happened. The *pulkka* rocked as one of the pack caught up and, with a mighty leap, jumped onto the racing *pulkka* and hung there behind Johan.

The leap had been so great that the animal struck the old man in the middle of the back, almost throwing him on his face. Even as he was being thrust forward and forced to release the rein, Johan somehow managed to half turn and swing his fist at the uninvited passenger. It was Veddge.

His fist took the dog full in the chest. Caught off balance, he was thrown out onto the snow; but his months of living alone in the wilds saved him. While an ordinary dog might have stayed for a moment to collect his scattered wits, Veddge bounded to his feet at once.

Two of the nearest wolves had swerved toward him, but he was too quick for them. With hardly a pause he went racing in pursuit of the *pulkka*. The wolves had divided into two teams of three. The she-wolf and her two youngest ran on one side of the *pulkka*, waiting for the reindeer stag to lose his first wild burst of speed. On the other side was the rest of the pack.

Veddge ran behind the *pulkka*. The seven animals were like an escort, one running behind to make sure no one escaped over the back of the *pulkka*, the others to stop the reindeer stag swerving to left or right.

After a minute Veddge had completely recovered from the shock of being tossed out onto the snow. Gathering himself for a mighty effort, he leaped once again onto the back of the fast-moving vehicle.

Johan felt the *pulkka* quiver and rock as the dog ascended. He shot a quick glance over his right shoulder and, easing the rein into his left hand, picked up his knife again. If he struck this dog a second time, it would not be with his fist, but with cold steel!

As if he realized the danger, Veddge remained perched at the back of the *pulkka*, watching Johan intently and occasionally stealing a glance first to one side, then to the other, so that he could make sure what the wolves were doing.

They were going down a slight slope now, into a valley. In the moonlight the snow-covered landscape seemed to stretch for endless miles into the distance. A few small birch trees broke the flatness, but that was all. It was the beginning of the Arctic winter, and this shimmering white would remain for months to come, the snow becoming deeper and deeper after each new storm.

Johan was nervous. He was afraid of the dog perched

on the back of the *pulkka,* and he was worried about his stag. Going downhill required little effort to drag the *pulkka* along, but Johan could tell that his reindeer was already beginning to falter. The splendid head was drooping.

"He's got to keep going," Johan muttered, and then with a grim little chuckle he murmured, "If I get out of this alive, what a tale it will be to tell. Wolves on each side of me, and a great, wild dog perched near enough behind me to snap my head off if it wanted to."

He shot a longer glance at Veddge and for the first time noted what a powerful creature the dog was. He was a fit companion for wolves, though his jaws were heavier than those of a wolf. His tail was bushier too.

"Somebody lost him; then he went wild," Johan muttered, and with a shrug he added: "Though I never heard of a Lapp dog running with wolves. Wonder if he knows any commands?"

Keeping his knife ready, he half turned and spoke to Veddge: "Come here, boy; come here." It was not a coaxing tone he used, but the command of a man to a dog who works for him. For a few moments Veddge gave no sign that he had heard the words.

Johan spoke to him again, and this time the bushy tail wagged a little, and the emerald green eyes blinked. The tail wagged once more when Johan spoke again, and then there was something else to occupy the old man's thoughts. His stag was slowing down. The long, loping stride that had taken them down the slope at a speed which had

§ 101

stretched the wolves to a fast gallop had suddenly slowed to little more than a canter. They were off the long slope, on level ground. Now the reindeer stag had not the strength to haul the *pulkka* at any real speed.

Fear of what might happen in the next minute sharpened Johan's wits. He turned again to Veddge, and now his voice was friendlier as he called him to come nearer. If he could get the dog on his side, there might be a chance. "Come here, boy; come here," he coaxed, and was rewarded with another friendly tail wag. Then Veddge barked. It was a bark, not a snarl, and a moment later he moved down to the old man, almost upsetting the *pulkka* as he pushed Johan off balance.

"You fool," Johan growled, thrusting the dog from him, and as he did so, the *pulkka* swerved and slid to a stop. In those few moments while Johan had been trying to make friends with Veddge, the she-wolf had come alongside the panting reindeer stag and made a feint leap at the animal's throat.

Swerving to avoid the attack, the stag almost trampled a wolf on the other side. He had to stop, and the *pulkka* slid to rest. Desperately the stag reared and hit out at his attackers, but he was tired and slow. His hoofs merely threshed the air, and the wolves avoided him without trouble.

The she-wolf came in, and now she really meant business. If she could get a grip on the stag's throat, or even on his nose, it would be the beginning of the end.

Forgetting that the dog beside him was not one of his

§ 102

own herd dogs, Johan yelled the command that would send any herd dog to the rescue of a reindeer being attacked. Veddge had not heard that command since the time he had been so unceremoniously tipped off Aslak's *pulkka*, months earlier. But he remembered and obeyed.

With a yelping snarl he leaped off the *pulkka* and flung himself to the defense of the floundering stag. Within seconds the night that had been so silent was noisy with yelps and howls as the rest of the wolves flung themselves onto the dog. They had a score to pay, and there was no drawing back now.

The fight should have been over in half a minute, for Veddge was outnumbered six to one; yet he had several advantages. The greatest of these was that he could bite and slash at anything near. The wolves had to make sure whom they were biting, or risk injuring one another. In their frantic eagerness brother bit sister, and the she-wolf slashed at more than one of her own family. Veddge was not getting off scot-free, but he was putting up a tremendous fight when Johan came to his assistance.

The old man was not deliberately helping Veddge. He was taking this chance of getting rid of one or more wolves while they were busy trying to kill this unknown dog.

Knife in hand he rushed across, the moonlight shining silver bright on the steel blade as it swung up and then down. There was a death howl and a wolf rolled over, kicking.

Johan slashed again, but this time his aim was not so

good. The wolf he tried to kill rolled over even as the knife came down, for Veddge was biting on the wolf's right forepaw.

The blade missed the wolf, and it was Johan who howled. He had put so much power in the thrust that when the point missed its aim, it swung down and sliced through his reindeer leggings into his leg. In that moment of disaster, those who thought the old man was fit only for riding a *pulkka* or drinking brandy at a wedding would have been enlightened.

Injured though he was, Johan struck again and again. Sometimes the knife found a target, sometimes it missed. The fight lasted no more than fifty seconds, for suddenly the remaining wolves seemed to realize that another enemy had arrived.

There was a flurry of legs and bodies as the wolves scattered. Two remained on the bloodstained snow. Both were dead.

Veddge was sprawled on the snow, and when Johan bent to see if the dog was alive, he had to whip his hand back like lightning, or he would have had his fingers bitten off. Veddge had snapped at him, then sprang to his feet ready to defend himself.

"You fool," Johan roared. The voice did something to Veddge. Seconds before, he had been fighting for his life and biting at anything within reach. Now the voice of Johan steadied him. His tongue lolling out, his flanks heaving as he fought for breath, he looked up at the old man.

Then his tail wagged for an instant as if he were trying to thank the old man for saving him.

Johan looked at the wolves. Like Veddge, they were panting for breath. Like him, they were bleeding, but for the moment they were content to wait and see what would happen next. If the old man had not interfered, they would have torn Veddge to pieces; but the old man was still there, glaring at them.

"You are a fighter," Johan murmured admiringly, and stooped to lay a hand on the young dog's head. The movement brought a gasp of pain from Johan. In the excitement of the past few minutes, he had forgotten the wound he had given himself. Bending had tightened the muscles, sending a pain shock up his leg. He put a hand down to the reindeer-skin trouser leg and realized he had hurt himself badly.

Hurriedly he wiped his hand on his sleeve and looked anxiously across at the wolves. He knew from experience that a wolf had to be very near starvation before it would attack a human being, but he felt certain these wolves had reached that point. They were very hungry, and the smell of blood could excite them even more.

"Come on," he said brusquely, and turned to climb into the *pulkka*—only there was no *pulkka* to climb into! While the wolves had been attacking Veddge, the tired reindeer stag had summoned up sufficient strength to start a slow trot south. Like his master, the stag was afraid of the wolf pack, and now he was a hundred and fifty yards away, seen only as a faint blur on the moonlit snow.

"Fetch him, fetch him," Johan ordered, realizing that with his injured leg he could not hope to overtake the reindeer.

At the word "fetch," which in the Lapp tongue is *veddge*, the dog wagged his tail. It was the first time he had heard his name in months, and it excited him so that his eyes glowed with delight.

Johan repeated the command: "Fetch him. Fetch him!" Then he swore in disgust when Veddge's only response was a delighted tail wagging. "Tcha! You are no Lapp dog," the old man growled, then turned to look anxiously toward the remaining wolves. One of them had gotten to its feet and stood staring fixedly at Johan. It was so hungry that it was desperate enough to risk death and again start a fight that had already left two of the pack dead on the snow.

When the she-wolf also rose, Johan knew he had to do something at once. She was limping, and her wounds were already beginning to stiffen; but her eyes showed cold, terrible hatred.

"Follow me and you'll get this," Johan threatened, swinging the knife in a wide arc in the hope that the cold light of the moon shining on the steel would make the wolves hesitate. The she-wolf did slink back a pace, not because of the steel, but at the voice. She was old enough to know that man was an enemy to be feared.

Johan started to limp south, and Veddge followed at his heels. He too was limping. He had no serious wounds, but the bites he had received were already beginning to stiffen.

§ 107

Trying to think of some way to stop the bleeding, and at the same time to protect the wound from the bitter cold, Johan suddenly remembered the braid binding about his ankles. This was wrapped over the top of the reindeer-hide shoes and the bottom of the trousers. It protected the ankles and kept snow from getting into the shoes.

Bending down and keeping a wary eye on the wolves, Johan untied one of the three-inch-wide strips. He bound it about his injured leg. It was rough-and-ready first aid, but he was hoping that it would stop the bleeding.

The wolves watched every movement he made. When he stopped walking, they stopped. When he started again, they followed. In some way the she-wolf knew he was hurt; and an injured man, like an injured animal, grows gradually weaker if he cannot rest. The she-wolf was content now to wait until exhaustion made Johan collapse.

After twenty minutes Johan was staggering a little. He stopped, and scooping up a handful of snow, he put some in his mouth. He rolled it round his tongue until it melted and was warm enough for him to swallow. He knew better than to gulp it down in its half-frozen state. Though it would have refreshed his parched throat, it could have brought him down with stomach cramps.

Veddge watched every move anxiously. He too guessed there was something wrong with Johan and sensed why the wolves were content just to follow. They were ready to play a waiting game. The time to rush him would be when Johan collapsed.

The old man managed to walk on unsteadily for

another fifteen minutes. Then he dropped to one knee. He rested like that for several minutes while Veddge walked slowly to and fro between him and the four wolves. They were growing impatient. They were half starved, and the smell of blood was spurring them to do something immediate. It was the she-wolf who kept them from rushing in.

After kneeling for a minute or so, occasionally shaking his head in an effort to clear the dizziness which threatened him, Johan stretched a hand down into the snow. His mouth was so hot and dry, and his head seemed to be on fire. Perhaps another mouthful of snow would help. At least it would be cold!

He had not realized how weak and shaky he was, for as he scooped a hand into the snow, he lost his balance and flopped full length. It brought a chorus of anxious, eager whines from the wolves as they pressed a little closer.

Veddge advanced a pace, snarling a warning. They stopped, watching as Johan tried to get to his knees. He knew he had to get on his feet at once—or die. Even if the wolves did not kill him, the cold could finish him off. Veddge whined anxiously. There was nothing he could do except keep the wolves off.

Three times Johan almost heaved himself onto his knees, but each time he toppled over. He was muttering to himself, but the words were little more than a whisper. He had lost a lot of blood, and his strength was gone. He hardly knew what he was doing, and only his iron will made him struggle.

§ 109

No man could have fought more gallantly than did Johan that night. Four times he struggled to get to his knees, four times his strength was not enough and he slid back into the snow. Then he lay still, a helpless old man, unable to summon up strength to make a further move.

Veddge stared at him for a few moments, half expecting him to try again. Then he put a paw on Johan's shoulder and, standing there, faced the wolves. The coarse hair on his neck and shoulders stood up like a ruff. He was growling deep in his throat, daring the wolves to come even one step closer. One of the younger wolves turned his muzzle to the moonlit sky and made the night hideous with a blood-chilling howl. When he finally stopped, Veddge replied with a fierce barking that made his whole body shake. He seemed to be saying: "Howl, and I'll bark. I'm not afraid."

He fell silent after half a minute, for the wolves had slowly separated. One moved round behind him. There was one on his left side, one on his right side, and one in front of him. They were not going to rush him from the front. One would dash in from one side, and while he was meeting that attack, the one behind him would dash in and perhaps nip him in the hindquarters. Wolves have been using this kind of attack for centuries, and it usually succeeds.

The she-wolf started the attack. She came in with a snarling rush, but swerved to one side as Veddge inched forward to meet her. As she did that, the wolf behind him leaped in. The teeth failed to close on Veddge's hindleg, but clamped hard on the tip of his tail.

§ 110

Veddge swung round and almost fell as the wolf refused to release the tail grip. This was the moment the others had been waiting for, and they advanced with a grimly silent rush.

In a moment the battle was on and the silence completely shattered. As the wolves piled in on him, Veddge rolled onto his back, the better to defend himself. There were snarls and whines and sudden howls of pain, but this time Veddge had to fight alone. There was no man to help him, for Johan lay on the snow limp and silent.

"Where is the dog?"

If he had only been able to stagger on for another three quarters of a mile, Johan would have reached the encampment where his daughter Susannan, his grandson Aslak, and their two herdsmen had pitched their tent. The herd of reindeer were scattered across the valley sleeping, almost invisible in the snow.

Down toward the herd went Johan's big stag, drawing the empty *pulkka* at a very slow trot. He reached the fringe of the herd. At once sleeping reindeer began to rise and move away.

A light breeze was blowing up the valley, and it carried with it the scent of woodsmoke. It was the smell of burning birch that drew Johan's stag to the tiny encampment. He knew that woodsmoke meant men, and men spelled safety. The smell of woodsmoke gave him strength enough to plod on through the disturbed reindeer herd until a dog began to bark.

To the barking of the dog was added the angry shouting of a man. The Lapp herdsman had been contentedly smoking a pipe on the far fringe of the sleeping herd when

§ 113

his dog gave the alarm. Trained to notice anything unusual, the dog had seen the movement as the stags, does, and calves rose uneasily to allow the *pulkka* to pass.

Cocking his rifle, the herdsman hurried through the disturbed reindeer and was ready to fire if he caught sight of a hunter. He was expecting to see the dark, squat body of a wolverine and gaped in amazement when Johan's big reindeer stag came slowly by, dragging the empty *pulkka*.

Within seconds the alarm had been given. Nor was there any need for explanations when Susannan and Aslak hurried from the little tent. The empty *pulkka* and the exhausted state of the reindeer stag were enough. Something terrible had happened to Johan.

There was nothing they could do for the big stag. He lay there, his eyes glazed and his flanks heaving. He needed rest, but his master might already be dead. They had to try to find him.

To the herdsmen Susannan said: "Follow the *pulkka* tracks back. Under this moon it should not be difficult, and I'm sure my father cannot be far away. His stag didn't know we were down here, so he must have gotten the scent of smoke from our fire and followed that. If you need help, fire three shots and I'll come with a *pulkka*."

The two men began to ski through the uneasy herd of reindeer while Aslak rushed back to the tent for his rifle. Pocketing a handful of cartridges, he slipped his feet into the loops of his skis and sped after the men. He caught up with them as they reached the fringe of the herd, for the reindeer had parted to let them through.

In the moonlight it was fairly easy to see the tracks of the reindeer stag and the *pulkka*, for the snow was soft and the tracks were deep. They made the best speed they could over the soft snow, and after hurrying up the valley for about five minutes, they stopped when Aslak called: "Did you hear that? It sounded like a dog barking."

"You are mistaken," one of the men insisted. "Our herd is the only one around here, and you don't get dogs traveling this country unless they are with a herd."

"You are wrong," Aslak insisted. "I heard a dog barking—barking angrily."

All three stopped and listened, and in the silence came another sound. It was not the barking of a dog but the blood-chilling sound made by a wolf as it howls to the moon. After a few moments it stopped, and then came the defiant barking of a dog.

"I said I'd heard a dog," Aslak shouted, and swinging his ski sticks, he moved forward, the two herdsmen at his heels. They stopped again a few moments later, for after the barking of the dog came a sound entirely different. It was like that of the greatest dog fight ever. There were howlings and screeches, shrill yelps of pain and snarls of anger. The sound came over the silent snows as clearly as if it had come from just beyond the rise.

Aslak skied then as he had seldom skied before. A terrible fear was clutching at his heart; fear for his grandfather. He had a sudden mental picture of old Johan fighting for his life, with a whole wolf pack piling in on him. Aslak's heart was cold as he raced up the snow slope.

§ 115

"Over here!" he yelled, for in the white brilliance of the moon he had caught a glimpse of a dark patch on the snow ahead. The two men with him knew the best way of dealing with wolves. Without bothering to take aim, they fired their rifles, reloading swiftly as they followed Aslak. The thunder of the firing did the trick.

The dark patch ahead suddenly spread out. The wolves had long ago learned what the roar of a rifle meant, and they began to run, leaving an ominously still shape stretched out on the snow.

Bang . . . bang . . . bang! Three shots rang out. Two wolves collapsed, and a third rolled over. It got to its feet and began limping away, only to be brought down as two more shots rang out. The fourth wolf raced away into the night.

Two animals lay together as Aslak came up with a rush. He looked anxiously about and saw another shape on the snow a dozen yards away. Sick with fear he skied across and a moment later was kneeling by old Johan, shaking him gently and asking him to speak.

As the two men came up, one drew Aslak aside and bent to see if the old man was still alive.

"Is he dead?" Aslak asked, a quiver in his voice.

"I don't know. Be quiet," the Lapp ordered, and put his ear close to Johan's mouth. He was hoping to catch the sound of breathing; but it was only when he turned Johan so that his face looked up at the moonlit sky that he got any reward. There was a faint puff of white coming from the old man's mouth. It was his breath turning to vapor in the bitter cold. It gave the men new hope.

Turning to Aslak, one of the herdsmen said: "Aslak, go back to your mother. Tell her we have found him. Tell her to heat soup. Then come back with a *pulkka* and two reindeer. Be as quick as you can, and we'll try to rub some life into him while you are away."

Aslak sped off, his skis throwing a fine spray of dry snow on either side. Meanwhile the Lapp herdsmen tried to bring back some life to the still figure. One pummeled him about the shoulders and ribs, the other chafed his legs.

The man chafing Johan's legs discovered the blood-soaked bandage, and his face became grim as he thought the wound must be a wolf bite. A bite from a wolf could bring blood poisoning, and that *could* be fatal.

After fifteen minutes Johan began to show signs of returning consciousness. He groaned a little and tried to move. The two men, perspiring from their efforts, rubbed and pummeled even more vigorously.

They stopped for a moment when the old man opened his eyes and tried to struggle to a sitting position. They forced him gently back, saying: "Lie still, Johan. We are trying to help you."

"Help me!" Johan grunted, and there was a note of indignation in his voice when he added: "If you do . . . much more . . . you'll kill me. Let me . . . oh-oh . . . mind my right leg. It hurts."

"You must lie still!" one of the men insisted. "We've

§ 117

sent your grandson for a *pulkka*. With luck we'll have you back to the tent in a few minutes. Then we can look at the leg." He began once more to pummel and rub Johan's arms and chest.

When Aslak came back, driving two panting reindeer stags, he brought with him a kettle of hot soup. The soup had been boiling furiously when Aslak's mother took the kettle off the fire, and she had wrapped it in a reindeer robe in an effort to keep it warm. Aslak had hurried, but the bitter cold had already cooled the soup so that Johan could drink it without burning his mouth.

The old man was lifted to a sitting position, and a wooden cup filled to the brim was held to his lips. He swallowed it noisily and held the mug out for a refill. After drinking a second cupful, he sat with head bowed. The soup seemed to be warming him through and through.

"I'm ready," he finally said. "Help me onto the *pulkka*."

While Aslak held the lead reindeer, the herdsmen lifted Johan into the back of the flimsy-looking *pulkka*. They wrapped him with reindeer robes and were about to signal to Aslak to start when Johan asked: "Where is the dog?"

"Which dog?" The herdsmen and Aslak asked the question together. "There is no dog!"

"The big dog. The one which saved me," Johan said impatiently. "But for him I'd have been torn to pieces long ago. He must be here."

"You didn't have a dog, Grandfather," Aslak pointed

out. "Don't you remember? We wanted you to keep a dog when we left you days ago—but you refused."

"I've had a dog for hours," Johan growled. "Do you think I don't know what I'm talking about? Find him. He came with the wolves—and then changed sides and helped me."

The two herdsmen exchanged quick glances. They were sure Johan's injury and the exhaustion brought on by cold had made him delirious.

"We could look for the dog later," one of the men suggested. "It is best to get you down to the tent. You'll feel better by a fire, and we . . ."

"Look for the dog!" Johan bawled, and made to throw off the reindeer robes.

"Don't get up, Grandfather," Aslak pleaded. "I'll look." He hurried across to the two dark shapes sprawled one on top of the other.

He dragged the first one aside. It was a big she-wolf, already stiffening in death. He grabbed the foreleg of the other, meaning to pull it out of the mess of trampled snow, and his fingers closed on something very peculiar.

He lifted the leg a little and stared at a wrapping of dirt-crusted braid bound tightly about the animal's foreleg.

"Is it a dog?" one of the herdsmen asked.

Aslak did not answer. He dropped to one knee to better examine the bandaged leg. He did not recognize his puppy, but his mind had gone back to the previous spring. They had been about to start on the annual trek north to the Norwegian islands, and his young puppy Veddge had

§ 119

been hurt. As he knelt here, he remembered it all. His grandfather had told him to put the dog out of its misery, but because he was fond of the puppy, he had disobeyed. He had used a piece of his mother's colored braid to bandage the injured leg. Then, during a high storm, Veddge had vanished. How or why he had gone they did not know.

Aslak recalled how upset he had been, and then in the weeks that followed, he had forgotten all about the young puppy. He fingered the dirt-crusted braid wrapped about the dog's foreleg. This animal was no puppy but a splendid, almost full-grown dog. Then his grandfather broke into his thoughts with a gruff "Have you found him? What are you kneeling there for? Is it a dog?"

"Yes, Grandfather, it is a dog." Lifting the limp body as gently as he could, Aslak carried Veddge across to the *pulkka*. His grandfather looked at the dog and gave a triumphant "That's him! Is he alive? Cover him up."

"I think he's living," Aslak agreed. Laying a hand on the dog's ribs, he thought he could feel the heartbeat. Gently he covered the dog with a warm reindeer robe. Then he ran to the lead reindeer and started the *pulkka* down the valley. One of the herdsmen skied ahead to tell Susannan they were bringing her father in. The other man called his dogs and took up the night herding again. There might be other wolves about, and the reindeer must be watched.

No one but Aslak had time for the dog once the tent was reached. Johan was laid on reindeer hides and the frozen bandage cut gently away from the wound in his leg. While Susannan was doing that, Aslak did what he could for the dog. Veddge was not dead, but he was suffering from some ugly-looking bites. Though he had lost a lot of blood, he was still breathing.

When Aslak's mother later examined the dog, she shook her head. "I don't think you can do anything for him," she said soberly. "It would be cruel to keep him alive, and the best thing . . ."

"No!" Aslak said sharply, and when his mother gave him an angry look, he added hurriedly: "Mother, I'm sure he is Veddge, the puppy I lost. Look at the bandage we took off his leg. Isn't it the same kind of braid you were using to decorate a frock in spring? I was afraid you'd shout at me for taking a piece and using it on the puppy. I'm sure this is Veddge."

As if the sound of his name had somehow penetrated the dog's semiconsciousness, Veddge lifted his head and gave a little whimper.

"I'm sure we can save him," Aslak insisted. "When we lost him, you said he would soon be dead. I said that he was a fighter and would surely come back to us. I was right. This *is* my puppy Veddge—though he has now become a dog."

His mother did not say anything. She was more worried about her father than about a dog. She knew that unless they could get Johan into the hands of a doctor fairly soon, the wound on his leg might kill him. The only way to get help was to send one of the herdsmen south to the nearest settlement where there was a radio telephone.

Once the man had left, there was little they could do but wait and hope.

Two anxious days passed, and then there was a distant hum which grew into the roar of a small ski plane. The noise sent the browsing reindeer scampering away in terror, but for the moment no one worried about that. The flying doctor had arrived!

A quick inspection of Johan's injury confirmed what Aslak's mother had feared. Her father would have to go south to the hospital. Any further delay might mean the loss of his leg, or worse.

"Can we take the dog?" Johan asked as they were strapping him on a stretcher. "He needs a doctor as much as I do."

The doctor grunted before explaining: "For what it would cost to treat your dog, you could buy the best dog in the land. My advice is . . ."

"I don't want your advice," Johan interrupted. "I want you to agree to take my dog. Look at him and tell me if he can be saved."

Reluctantly the doctor examined Veddge. With a shrug he admitted that the dog's life could be saved; but he added the warning that it would cost more than the dog was worth.

"We'll take him," Johan said, smiling happily. "There are some dogs money can't buy, and he's one of them."

His words brought a relieved smile to Aslak's lips.

Veddge was carefully rolled in a reindeer robe and strapped so that he would not wriggle free. Then he was carried to the plane. A few minutes later, its engine thundering in the snowy quiet, the ski plane lifted into the air and flew south.

*　　*　　*

Seven weeks later when it was high summer and the days were so long that the sun was still shining at midnight, Johan returned. With him was a big, handsome dog who bounded along as if he had never known what a wolf bite meant. True, he had a slight limp, and his ribs and ears showed healed scars; but there was a gloss on his coat that told of perfect health. Whatever Johan had paid for Veddge's treatment in the hospital, the dog looked worth every penny of the money.

Veddge kept at Johan's heels until Aslak called: "Veddge!"

For a moment the dog seemed puzzled, as if he was searching his memory for that voice. Then he gave a deep bark of delight and hurled himself at Aslak, almost bowling him over.

"You'll not get lost again," Aslak assured him as he pushed the dog away, for Veddge was slobbering all over him, trying to lick his face and neck. "Come on, you can have a bite of food. Then you can start earning your keep. I'm off to the fell for a night's herding."

From the pot Aslak took a big bone with plenty of meat sticking to it. Veddge waited until the tidbit was cool enough. Then he grabbed it and followed his young master to where the reindeer were feeding on the moss-covered fells.

About the author

PETER HALLARD has written a number of successful adventure stories enjoyed by readers both in this country and abroad. He is chairman of the northern branch of the British Society of Authors. He travels extensively, and presently lives in Lancashire, England, with his wife, Elizabeth.

About the artist

WALLACE TRIPP has been a New Englander all his life and now lives in New Hampshire. This talented young artist has illustrated many children's books and is particularly well known for his portrayals of animal personalities.